COTTAGE IN THE COUNTRY

Amy inherits Rose Cottage, which is in a terrible state of repair. However, wanting to gain a share of its value, her relatives hope that she will refuse the bequest. But Amy keeps Rose Cottage, employing local architect Ben to overhaul the building. Despite living amid chaos during the transformation Amy is determined to stay. If only she could include Ben permanently in her life things would be perfect — but she's not the only one who likes Ben . . .

WENDY KREMER

COTTAGE IN THE COUNTRY

Complete and Unabridged

LINFORD
Leicester

First published in Great Britain in 2008

First Linford Edition
published 2010

34569545ᑫ

British Library CIP Data

Kremer, Wendy.
    Cottage in the country. - -
    (Linford romance library)
    1. Inheritance and succession- -Fiction.
    2. Cottages- -Remodeling- -Fiction.
    3. Architects- -Fiction. 4. Love stories.
    5. Large type books.
    I. Title II. Series
    823.9′2–dc22

    ISBN 978–1–44480–415–7

Published by
F. A. Thorpe (Publishing)
Anstey, Leicestershire

Set by Words & Graphics Ltd.
Anstey, Leicestershire
Printed and bound in Great Britain by
T. J. International Ltd., Padstow, Cornwall

This book is printed on acid-free paper

1

'It's not really fair, is it?' Marie absentmindedly stroked the surface of the reception desk with her red-tipped fingers.

Amy Austin smothered a fitting response and wondered if it wouldn't be better just to give in. 'Blame Aunt Sally, Mary! Not me!'

'*Marie*, darling!' Her voice jumped an octave. 'I wish you wouldn't forget it, all the time! You know the press is very picky about actress's names!'

Mary had become *Marie* when she took up acting. Only one newspaper reporter had noted Marie's existence so far, and he was a local one.

'You don't have to accept, do you?' Marie's voice pleaded. 'If you refuse, we'd all get a share, wouldn't we? Then everyone will be happy.'

Amy shook some papers into a neat

pile, and tried not to sound put out.

'I don't honestly know. We'll wait and hear what the lawyer has to say on Saturday.'

A good-looking young man with corn coloured hair opened the entrance door and interrupted their conversation. 'Morning, Amy!' He gave Marie a polite smile.

Marie fluttered her eyelashes.

Amy smiled back. 'Hi! Had a good weekend?'

He nodded, and his smile widened. 'Great, and you?'

'Not bad!' Amy handed him his post for the day, and a list of telephone calls.

Nodding in acknowledgement he glanced at the list and his forehead furrowed. He started to flip through the envelopes as he sauntered towards his office.

Marie rolled her eyes. 'My, oh my! You do work with nice men, don't you? What's his name? Is he married? What does he do?'

Amy sighed, and wondered why Marie

did a metamorphosis and became Diana the Huntress the moment she saw an attractive man. 'He's Mike Bowers. He's engaged, he's a network technician, he also happens to own this business.'

'Umm! Interesting! What's a network technician? If you introduce us properly I bet I could get him to take me out for a meal in no time at all!'

Impatiently Amy replied. 'I'll do no such thing. I just told you he's engaged. A network technician establishes network users, installs, and upgrades systems, provides users with support . . .'

The computer language went in, and came straight out the other side of Marie's brain; she yawned artificially. Covering her scarlet mouth for a moment with fingertips that perfectly matched the colour of her lipstick, she stared wide-eyed at Amy and said. 'I'm sure that's utterly fascinating, if you know what it means but I must be off! I've managed to organise a lunch date with a very, very influential agent.

Think seriously about what'll happen if you accept, darling! . . . I'm only trying to be supportive.'

Amy liked Marie, despite the fact that they were so different. Amy tried to appreciate the positive aspects of her cousin's character and was prepared to compromise about the rest. She didn't take Marie seriously, and she didn't pay much attention to Marie's unasked-for opinions either.

* * *

Benjamin Tyler BA — Architectural Planning, Services and Valuations. Amy had often passed the brass sign before, but now she eyed it with hope. She pushed open the main door and went in. She rapped on the door a couple of times and then entered.

A man was bent over a lighted desk, busy with paperwork. His head lifted as she approached, and he straightened up. Standing head and shoulders above her, his face was partially obscured in

the fading daylight; he asked politely,
'Can I help you?'
'Mr Tyler?'
He nodded silently.
She was nervous, but it didn't show.
'My name is Amy Austin. I need someone to value a cottage I'm about to inherit from a great-aunt. I want to know how much it's worth; and how much it would cost to modernise it.'

He stuck a hand in one of the pockets of his soft brown corduroys. 'I see. I presume that you need a quick valuation?' He motioned with his free hand towards a chair with a sweeping gesture. 'Sorry, I'd like to help, but I don't honestly think I can take on a new commission at present. There's no point in me pretending otherwise.'

Amy flopped down feeling disappointed. Despite his obvious reluctance to help, she found herself explaining the whole story; how she was the main beneficiary, and how the rest of the family resented it.

His dark eyes twinkled in the

half-gloom. 'So you need to decide whether to keep it, and live with their wrath for ever more, or refuse what is legally yours?'

'Exactly! If I accept, I've got to live there and can't sell it for a couple of years; that's a stipulation. If I refuse, the cottage will be sold, and I suppose all of the family will then share whatever it's worth. The will is being read this Saturday, but I already know I'm the main beneficiary — my great-aunt told me years ago.'

His voice was sympathetic; his words were not. 'I'd like to help, really I would, but estimation takes time, and I'm just too busy at present.' He smiled briefly, and despite the meagre light Amy was able to see the upward sweep of his generous mouth and the flash of white teeth. 'One client is threatening because I promised him plans last weekend.' He pointed to the desk. 'They're still here because I'm bogged down with other work!'

Amy tried again; for some reason, she

wanted this man to do the job. When she made up her mind Amy was determined. 'I only want a rough idea! No detailed list or anything like that.'

He ran a hand over his face and then moved to the light-switch by the door. Amy blinked and focused again. He had an angular face, and well-shaped thick eyebrows framing dark eyes. His hair ended above the collar of his checked flannel shirt.

He studied her and liked what he saw. She was attractive and had a friendly face, his eyes swept over her approvingly. 'Where's it situated?'

Hope burgeoned; she rushed on. 'It's down a narrow lane leading off the new bypass to Lomsdon. It's called *Rose Cottage*; it's been empty for years.'

He rubbed his chin and deliberated. 'Oh! Yes, I know it as a matter of fact. Slate roof, rough stonewall masonry, stone porch with a pitched roof, and a couple of small outhouses in a hedged garden. It used to have lovely old-fashioned wooden sash windows at one time.'

She was pleased and surprised that he knew the cottage so well and nodded enthusiastically. 'My father's aunt lived there until she moved to sheltered accommodation for the last years of her life.'

He nodded. 'I remember her; she used to be a teacher in the primary school.' Before she could ask anything, he added. 'I come from Lomsdon; my parents still live there.' He paused and ran his fingers through his thick hair; it sprung back obediently into place. 'I suppose I could pay them a long overdue visit, and take a look at the place while I'm there. I'd only be able to give you a very rough idea, and to be honest I don't really like cutting corners, because you need a professional assessment to make a serious decision, but I can see that it's probably difficult to make any kind of decision unless you can roughly guess what you're getting into.'

Amy was patently grateful, and said so.

Ben smiled. He mused that there was something special about Amy Austin and he was man enough to feel the attraction.

★   ★   ★

Mr Simpson, the lawyer, had made an exception; he'd arranged to meet them in his office on Saturday. It had proved impossible to get them all together on a weekday, if the first agreed the second couldn't, then the third could, and the first couldn't. He gave up, and decided it was easier to sacrifice an hour of his golf.

The atmosphere was strained. Amy studied them all as she sat on one of stiff high-backed chairs lining the walls of the stuffy room. There was her cousin, Thomas Copeland — Marie was the only one who'd ever dared to call him Tommy. He was a stockbroker in the city, a perfectionist who was determinedly investing towards a trouble-free old age.

He sat on the edge of his chair stiffly,

hands resting on his rolled umbrella, silently watching the cloudless blue sky outside the window. His mother, Aunt Jane, was a widow. She'd slipped into the role her husband had always played — of knowing exactly what to do, and what to say. She firmly, if wrongly, believed that the family thought she was a fountain of wisdom.

Uncle Walter brushed his bushy salt and pepper moustache upwards and shifted uneasily in his chair. He flicked bits of tobacco from his tweed trousers nervously, and checked his gold pocket watch again. An ex-military man, he loved punctuality.

Vera Phillips was Aunt Sally's cleaning lady. She'd hoped to inherit something. Amy didn't like her much. Vera sat primly, smiling weakly whenever she caught someone's eye.

Amy's mother was seated next to Amy; her quiet presence and warm smile helped to reassure Amy. On the other side of Amy was Marie. Today she looked totally out of place, in a gauzy leopard-spot blouse and skin-tight leather trousers. Marie checked her perfectly contoured lips in a small pocket mirror, before she threw it back into her over-sized bag in satisfaction, and closed it loudly with a snap.

Next to Marie was Marie's mother, Phyllis. Aunt Phyllis was a nervous being, with fluttering hands that never seemed to rest. She and Marie's father used to run a dancing school till he'd died suddenly, leaving Marie's mother with his life-insurance money. For the first time in her married life, Aunt Phyllis now had a reliable income. A lifetime of late nights and heavy make-up had left their spurs on her leathery skin.

The room was blanketed in silence. 'So ladies and gentlemen, Mrs Sally Austin's last will and testament is very straightforward. Miss Amy Austin inherits *Rose Cottage* with contents if she agrees to live there. If Miss Austin refuses the inheritance, or leaves the cottage within the space of five years, the value of the cottage is then to be divided between Jane Copeland, Thomas Copeland, Walter Austin, Phyllis Bennet, Mary Bennet, Susan Austin, Amy Austin and Vera Phillips.'

Aunt Jane did a quick calculation in her head and muttered loudly. 'Shared between eight people? How ridiculous! It would hardly be worth the bother.'

Vera Phillips pursed her lips as if she'd sucked a slice of lemon.

Thomas straightened his tie, and took out a pocket book to make notes.

Amy got up, avoided eye contact with the others, shook hands with the lawyer and made a quick exit. Aunt Jane had *organised* them to get together at the local pub, and Amy decided it was advisable to get a seat at the back of the room. Minutes later they were all in the lounge bar; luckily it was still too early for any of the local population.

Uncle Walter, his hand holding a pint of ale, started things off. He looked briefly at Amy. 'Nothing personal, my dear, but I think we should contest the will, so that we all get a share. Sally was always a bit odd.'

'Don't be ridiculous, Walter! Sally made that will years ago, before she moved. Her GP will confirm she was perfectly sane at the time.' Aunt Jane straightened her back and pointed her glass of sherry at her brother. 'Anyway, who pays for a court case? Not me, for one; no point in throwing good money after bad!'

'Quite right, Mother!' Thomas grasped his small whiskey and took measured sips. 'The cost would absorb any gain.'

Marie had positioned herself next to Amy, with a large vodka and lemon. She hissed meaningfully at Amy. 'See, what did I tell you? They're all at it, even though no-one even knows what the cottage is worth!'

Amy gripped her orange juice tighter and kept her voice down, but she sounded resolute. 'They're hypocrites. None of them cared about Aunt Sally. If Dad had inherited they wouldn't have made a fuss. Aunt Sally wasn't fond of any of them. She didn't even welcome you with open arms, did she?' Amy didn't want to sound spiteful, but she needn't have worried, Marie shrugged off the remark.

Her cousin lifted her chin. 'A true artist, like I am, is sensitive to criticism, Amy . . . Aunt Sally kept harping on about me doing something worthwhile whenever I called, so I stopped going. It was like visiting the vicar voluntarily to have your sins counted all the time! The only thing that anyone in this family really cares about is money.' She hesitated. 'Are you seriously thinking about moving there? It must be a pretty ghastly place now; closed up all these years — and it's so off the beaten track too.'

Amy wanted to get away from the family gathering; Marie gave her the idea of how to rescue the situation. 'I think I'll go and take a look.'

Marie gulped down the remaining liquid in her glass, slammed it on the table, and scrambled to her feet. 'Oh, goody! I'll come too.'

Amy looked down at her cousin's delicate pointed shoes. 'Marie, the quickest way is across fields — you won't enjoy walking cross-country in those! It rained yesterday; the fields are probably muddy!'

'Staying here won't be much fun either.' Looking around, she said, 'I'd rather brave the obstacles of the countryside than listen to this lot. I bet you they think I'm coming along just to find out if you're going to keep it or not! My phone will be red hot tomorrow.'

Amy realised that it wasn't far from the truth. Marie was extremely curious by nature, and when she gathered any interesting information she passed it on, in full and post-haste. Amy gave her a top to toe sweeping glance. 'You're not dressed for a country excursion, so if you come, don't blame me!' She got up and touched her mother's arm briefly. 'Will you be all right? If you'd like to come, I'll drive us all there in the car.'

Her mother shook her head. 'You're old enough to make up your own mind.' She looked around. 'This family is a nightmare! When your grandfather died the same thing happened; they fought about your grandfather's gold watch that time. Your granddad knew Walter loved antiques, so he left him the pocket watch, and the rest of them went haywire. Now you'd think the cottage was Blenheim Palace the way they're behaving. I'll ignore them, have a sandwich, and you can collect me later, OK?' She patted Amy's hand.

'Won't be too long, promise!' Amy left quietly, trying not to attract attention and ignoring people's faces on the way. Marie followed close on her heels, slipping into a tight-fitting waist-length black leather jacket as she went. On the wrong person, the outfit might have looked common, but on Marie it looked classy.

The shortcut went from behind the ancient church in a shallow curve along the boundaries of some fields. Ten minutes later Amy was wondering yet again why she'd let Marie come. The sun was high and a soft breeze made it a pleasant walk, but Marie grumbled non-stop about the distance.

Amy was relieved to see the cottage chimneys at last, but she was already dreading the return journey — and Marie's complaining remarks.

2

The once cared-for garden was submerged beneath weeds, shrubs and a wilderness of indefinable plants. A climbing rose bush, that used to frame the small porch-way with huge pale pink blooms, had run to seed and was now a mass of angry thorns on wiry stems.

The windows were hidden beneath nailed weathered boards, and the outhouses were all covered by rampaging ivy. Amy looked up and saw there were tiles missing from the roof; a couple of them were sticking out perilously from the guttering. A bench in a sheltered corner of the garden had fallen to moss-covered pieces, and the privet hedge had completely lost any claim to neat proportions.

Marie stared in horror. 'Good heavens; this is Aunt Sally's cottage? I can't believe it! Amy, you'd be mad to move in.'

Amy gulped, and had to admit it looked pretty daunting. She opened her mouth to answer, but was distracted by Ben Tyler as he came around the angle of the building. Today he looked very relaxed and at ease; one hand was stuck into a pocket of washed-out blue jeans, and a crisp white shirt peeped out from a navy-blue fisherman's jersey.

Amy bit her lip, and said quickly, 'Ben! Hello! I forgot you might be here!'

Marie's eyes widened, she looked at him then at Amy, and waited expectantly.

Amy obliged. 'Oh, Marie, this is my friend, Ben. We were talking about the cottage the other day. He was curious and wanted to see it for himself.' Amy's brain was whizzing. She didn't want Marie to know who Ben was yet. She wanted to decide about keeping the cottage or not, unhampered by warnings, proposal or alternative suggestions from anyone . . . especially from Marie.

He smiled knowingly. His face was slightly tanned from the wind and the sun; Amy surmised that he must spend a lot of time outdoors. A breeze ruffled his hair, and tiny crow's feet appeared at the corner of his brown eyes as he smiled and his glance roamed from one woman, to the other. 'Hi Amy!' He inclined his head towards Marie. 'Hello!'

Marie did the *Diana the Hunter* metamorphosis again. 'Ben? Amy's never mentioned you before. Been together long?'

Ben looked across briefly at Amy, and joined in the pretence. 'No, not long.'

Marie didn't beat about the bush. 'What do you do for a living, Ben?'

Amy knew how infinitely important this kind of information was to Marie.

Without blinking an eyelid, Ben replied. 'I'm in the building trade.'

Marie wasn't impressed with the answer, but she was with him. 'I must say Amy's taste is improving! The last one was a drip, a complete and utter disaster. I warned her about going out with a mechanic; the only things they're good for is repairing things, but she wouldn't listen.' She gave him a melting smile and her eyelashes flapped.

Amy considered knocking her sideways with her elbow, but she smiled stiffly instead and looked apologetically at Ben. She noted how his eyes took Marie in swiftly, and although he didn't seem to take much notice, Amy guessed he had already summed her up completely. Without commenting, he took Amy's arm with gentle authority. 'I've already had a quick look, but now you're here, we can take another stroll.'

They walked carefully, avoiding overgrown bushes, forlorn plants, and the debris of several years of neglect. General decay had turned a pretty cottage into a forlorn building. Most of the things Ben pointed out were obvious, but he also listed some aspects Amy hadn't thought about. Eventually Amy dawdled; throwing fallen branches to the side, and lost in memories of how the cottage had been in better times. She found herself following the other two.

Marie had her arm tucked through Ben's. She was chatting away to him nineteen to the dozen. Ben seemed to be enjoying her company.

When they reached the porch of the cottage, Marie said. 'Amy darling, as you have to pick up your mother to drive her to the station, and Ben is here on his own with his car, would you mind if he gives me a lift back to town?' A few steps away, Ben was silently examining one of the loose drainpipes.

Amy swivelled slowly away from them both, and looked briefly across a neighbouring field, brushing a cobweb of disappointment from her sleeve. 'No . . . of course not! Be my guest!'

Marie gave her a hasty kiss on her cheek. 'You're an angel! I was dreading that trek back through the fields.'

Normally Amy would have quipped and said she was too, but she didn't feel like joking any more. Ben's low voice cut in on her thoughts.

'I'll drop you off at the pub first. It's a bit of a squeeze on the back seat of the car, but I expect that Marie will manage.'

Amy was used to seeing how men reacted to Marie, and she sighed silently. 'No, carry on! I enjoy walking. Will you call me, or shall I come around on Monday?'

'Come round, by all means!'

She saw them off at the gate; it hung crookedly and its hinges were rusted. Marie got into his bottle-green car and leaned out to wave goodbye. It roared off along the tarred surface of the road.

Amy wondered what Marie's strategy would be; Marie didn't have a steady boyfriend at the moment. Amy strode out across the fields, busy with her thoughts. She looked up at the sky, clouds were gathering. Ben Tyler was old enough, and big enough, to take care of himself.

Marie's impulsive, gregarious nature

was something Amy secretly admired. Marie could grab and hold the attention of most men. Her looks attracted them, and the ability to handle them, kept them dangling. In comparison, Amy wasn't so successful even though her boyfriends had often been very nice men, but she'd never found one who'd set her pulses flying.

On Monday, Amy thought Ben's office might be closed during the lunch-hour, so she decided to call on her way home. He stood up when she came in. This time the room was brightly lit, and he flexed his arms briefly as though he'd been bent over too long in the same position; his shirt pulled dangerously across his shoulders as he did so.

'Ah! That's good! I've an appointment in an hour's time.' He motioned her towards a facing chair.

Amy sat down and she watched him settle on the corner of the desk; his legs crossed and his large hands gripping the edge. He held her glance. 'Well

. . . on the basis of what I saw Saturday, and I've got to do some guessing here, I estimate it needs a new drainage system, the roof needs some tiling, the windows and doors have to be replaced, and you might need new flooring. Does it have central heating?'

'No, that's one of the things Aunt Sally never got round to.'

'Then you also need a new heating system, and the place probably needs rewiring too.' Seeing the dismay in her face, he tried to console her quickly. 'The cottage has great potential; and considering its age, it's in good condition.'

She swallowed hard, as she absorbed his words. 'That . . . that sound's like a lot of investment money. And there could be other snags you haven't yet seen?'

'Well yes, that's a possibility of course. I won't be able to say for certain until I've had a look at the inside. You may be able to cut corners by ignoring some things for a while, but you're only putting off the inevitable. I see the same thing all the time; older people can't stand upheaval and don't want to get into debt, so they put off improvements and modernisation.

'Trouble is, every building needs care from time to time to remain sound, and to keep up its value. Your aunt was happy with less than perfect conditions, but I don't think you would be for long; you've grown up with modern facilities.' He paused. 'It won't fetch much on the market in its present condition either, it's too run-down and isolated, but if you modernise it, you'll have a comfortable home, and a good investment for the future. Or, once it's modernised, it'd sell like a hot-cake locally, or even to someone from further away who's looking for a weekend cottage.'

Amy thought about her meagre savings and felt depressed. 'I can only sell it after I've lived there for five years. Can I do any of the work myself?'

He got up, moved back behind the

desk and tried to sound sympathetic. 'Not much, I'm afraid. Most of the work is for specialists. Do you know how to install central heating, make doors and windows, or do roofing? Perhaps you could manage some decorating work yourself, it depends how good you are at that sort of thing, but . . . '

Her hands twisted unconsciously together. 'Would you be able to handle the conversion, if I decide to keep it?'

He didn't understand why he didn't refuse outright. 'Well . . . if you give me a couple of weeks to get some other projects out of the way . . . and it would still depend on exactly how much work is involved. I need a closer look inside to judge.'

'Can you then estimate what it would cost? A rough estimate of course!'

He ran his hand over his face. 'Very rough. I can only use my own ideas to do that. I'll be able to work out an exact one once you decide what you want to do.'

Amy nodded and got up. 'I'll get the key from the solicitor, and bring it round. If you're not here I'll drop it through the letterbox. I don't want to push you, but I hope you can find time as soon as possible to make a rough guess, because I only have a limited time to say yes or no.' Her voice was soft and polite. 'I'd be very grateful. I know you said before that you're very busy at the moment.'

He nodded silently then looked at her, puzzled by his own thoughts. 'You're completely different from Marie, aren't you? She's so impetuous and explosive, and you're quiet and sensible. It's hard to believe you're cousins.'

He was unaware that she picked up his comment in an uncomplimentary way. Amy flushed, glad that the conversation was at an end. Marie had won yet another admirer. She gave him a hesitant smile. 'Yes! People often say that!'

'The only thing that stopped her eating me alive on Saturday was the fact that she believes we're close friends.'

She gave him a stiff smile. 'I expect you coped very well!'

He smiled back and then looked at his watch; the metal casing caught the light. 'I'll be in touch with you after I've had a look inside!'

Amy's lips felt stiff as she tried to smile. She drew up the collar of her coat, pushed errant strands of hair out of sight, and adjusted her scarf. 'Thanks! I won't keep you any longer. Goodnight, Mr Tyler!'

'Let's stick to Ben and Amy, please! It's much nicer.'

She got up quickly, and hurried to the door without a backward glance.

Later, the bank manager studied her papers. 'Well, we'll have to weigh up all the pros and contras, but you've done your homework, and I don't see any great difficulty.'

Amy nodded, adding, 'I have a secure job. My mother will act as a guarantor if you need one. I see it as a long-term solid investment for my future.'

'Hmm!' He continued to peruse the

details. 'I see that you're hoping to use Ben Tyler? He has a good reputation, and does quality work. I'll pass this on to Mr Dawson; he handles house mortgages and loans. There are various finance plans, it's best for you to find out from him which one is most suitable, and how high the repayments will be.'

Amy nodded. He took off his glasses. 'I remember your aunt; she had an account with us for many, many years. When I was a young trainee clerk, she always had a pleasant word for me.' He got up. 'We'll make an appointment with Mr Dawson now.'

Mr Dawson gave her solid advice on various loans, helped her understand the complexities of a rate that would stand the test of time — one that accounted for what happened if she became unemployed or had a long illness. After absorbing that information, it was easy for Amy to opt to keep the cottage. Even if Ben, or anyone else, had advised against it, by now Amy would have fought the devil to keep it. The prospect of owning her own house, and the good memories she had of *Rose Cottage* swept any misgivings she might have had aside.

Ben had taken the boards down from the door and windows, and Amy had gone to see it herself again. She recalled the visits she'd made with her mother and father, tea in the garden, her aunt's all enveloping welcoming hugs whether she was a little girl or a grown woman — it all brought a lump to her throat and dissolved any last shreds of doubt.

3

Ben called, to present her with his estimation of the cost. She glanced gingerly at his figures. 'I don't want to change too much, if possible, Ben.'

Amy was expecting his amused expression — he knew she didn't have the slightest clue about what modernising *Rose Cottage* meant in actual work. His eyes twinkled.

'That's fine; as long as there's no reason I'm forced to change the structure in some way. I've a couple of suggestions to make though.'

'For instance?' Amy didn't want him to decide it all. It was going to be her home; if changes were on the line, he'd have to explain what and why.

'Well, for example, I thought it might be a good idea to integrate the adjoining outhouse, as part of the main cottage. It'd make a tremendous difference to the amount of your actual living space.'

Amy knew it was a great idea. The man didn't just look good; he knew what he was doing! 'Umm! Sounds fine.'

He glanced at his watch. 'Sorted out the finances?'

'Yes.'

He was silent for a second. 'So — are you going to keep it, or not?'

Amy looked at him steadfastly and took a deep breath. 'Yes. I went back again on the weekend. It's neglected, but it would make a great home.'

'I agree.' He gave her a generous smile. 'You'll face the family's wrath?'

His smile had a strange effect on her brain; she swallowed hard. 'Oh, I hear they've more or less adjusted! Cousin Tommy just wants more investment money, Uncle Walter was hoping for some extra cash to buy antiques, Aunt Phyllis wanted to go on a winter cruise, and the others were just gently hoping. I expect they'll now all hope I'll quit. If I do, within five years, they'll pounce on me like hyenas.'

The corner of his mouth twitched. 'And you don't care about the ghost?'

'What ghost?' Amy's eyes widened.

'Oh, just village gossip, I expect. My mother mentioned that there's a rumour that the cottage is haunted.'

With more defiance that she felt, Amy retorted. 'Nonsense! Aunt Sally never mentioned anything of the sort, and I don't believe in ghosts!'

He laughed, and his white teeth flashed briefly. 'Good. I don't believe in that stuff either.' He closed the folder in his hands and hitched it under his arm. He tilted his square chin. 'That's your copy of what I estimate, and the work I suggest. Study the figures carefully, so that you see what you're getting into. And if you take my advice you'll add a bit for unexpected costs too. Now that I know you've made up your mind, I'll try to get some rough sketches done this week.'

Amy made some plans of her own. She handed in notice on her flat, reckoning that although the cottage wouldn't be comfortable for a while, if she moved as soon as possible, she'd save a couple of months rent towards the coming expenditure.

Ben was horrified when she told him; his eyes widened and his eyebrows rose. 'Have you any idea of what that means? The inconvenience, the dirt, the dust, the noise, and how cold it will be until the heating is installed? It still has an outside toilet!'

She tossed her hair and her eyes glinted dangerously. 'Somehow, I thought you'd say that! My saved rent will go towards costs, so I'll put up with the inconvenience. If I live there, I'm on hand to keep an eye on things.'

'That's my job! You won't even have a bathroom until we've sorted out the drainage! Do you realise that you'll have to wash in a bowl in the kitchen, and use that primitive outside lavatory — even at night.'

'Aunt Sally had a tin bath, and managed with coal fires all her life; so I'll manage too. The sooner you get going, the sooner I'll be able to enjoy proper facilities.'

'You know that your cottage isn't the only job on my books; and this sort of thing takes time to organise.'

'Then I'll wait; or would you rather that I look around for someone else?' She didn't feel as confident as she sounded, but she met his eyes with determination.

He admired her grit and noted the tone of her voice. 'I'll take it on, of course. I'd like to — it's an interesting task!'

'Right!' Amy turned away to look out of the window. 'When can we start?'

'When are you planning your move?'

'In six weeks.'

He scratched his head, whistled softly, and was quiet for a moment. 'I'll do my best to get the roof done by then. By the way, if you intend to utilise the attic in the future, say so now! I'll need to take that into account.'

Registering her puzzled look, he explained. 'If you put in some dormer windows, it'll be ready for a loft conversion later on. You may as well let the roofing company do it all in one go now. An alternative would be two small casement windows in the gables. The cottage is relatively small, and you may be glad of an additional guest room, or bedroom, in the future — children need their own space.'

This time, Amy's eyes widened. 'Children? What children?'

He said flippantly. 'That's what I'm paid for — individual planning for present and future eventualities.'

The men from the roofing company were still clearing up their debris. Amy looked up at the finished work. The roofing company had only needed to fill in gaps, and replace damaged slates with new ones. Luckily they'd confirmed there was no damage to the wooden supporting frame.

Amy decided the cost of dormer windows didn't justify their possible benefits; so two new nine-pane casement windows were going into the end gables instead. She might never marry or have children, and Ben had said that a small window in each end wall would provide enough natural light for any small room.

She was pleased with the improved appearance; the roof looked neat and tidy with its new guttering and the chimney had been newly pointed. The men shouted a friendly goodbye, leaving her alone with her cottage; she felt extraordinarily possessive. The rest of the building was still a mess, but it was a start.

She decided to spend the weekend getting the cottage into a habitable state so that she could gradually bring her own things over every evening after work in the coming week. The door creaked as she entered and she wrote oil down on her shopping list.

A couple of hours later the upstairs rooms looked a lot better than when she'd arrived, and she decided to attack the downstairs tomorrow. She thought about staying overnight, but she had nothing to eat or drink and she felt too grubby. Looking around she decided a good clean up would improve the furniture no end, but the curtains, carpets, and other materials had suffered badly from neglect and moisture. It all smelled musty and mouldy.

★   ★   ★

Amy was just about to put out the light.

Marie's voice was loud and unbelieving. 'You're going to bed? But it's only ten-thirty, and it's Friday! I thought we could meet up and go to that new place out near Wiltbury. I'm sure Ben would enjoy it.'

'Ben?'

'Darling, has someone hit you with a hammer or something? Ben — your boyfriend, Ben!'

'Oh, Ben. Well, actually . . . he's not my boyfriend.'

'Amy, don't tell me you let him get away! For once in your life you picked someone decent, and you bungled it?'

'I . . . Ben was never my boyfriend.'

Amy explained. 'He's an architect. I went to him for his professional help, to decide whether to keep the cottage or not.'

'He's an architect?' She paused. 'You mean he's going to do the work on the cottage?'

'Umm!'

'You're nuts, Amy! Why didn't you just say who he was, and what he did, from the start? Why all the secrecy?'

'I wanted to decide without any distractions from you. I hadn't made up my mind.'

'So he's up for the taking? . . . Or are you interested in him in a non-professional way? Despite what everyone thinks, I do have some principles, I wouldn't barge in on your territory!'

'Me, interested in Ben? No, whatever gave you that idea?'

'He's attractive, male and single. What other reason does anyone need?'

Amy didn't want to think too much about Ben. 'Be my guest!'

'Really! Oh goodie! I'll keep that in

mind. Coming tonight?'

'No, I'm dog tired. I cleaned out part of the cottage this afternoon, and I'm going back tomorrow to do some more. I'm moving in next weekend.'

'Oh, yes — forgot about that; you must be mad! Tell you what, I'll come and help you tomorrow.'

'That's good of you, but . . . '

'No buts! Blood is thicker than water and all that, and I don't have any rehearsals tomorrow. What time?'

'I want to start early!' Amy knew that Marie would rather drink poison than get up early.

'Carry on! You can pick me up later! What can I do?'

Amy was already thinking wildly. Marie wouldn't do anything that endangered her nail polish; and she was the least domesticated person Amy knew. Even if Amy could persuade her to wash dishes Marie would probably end up breaking something. She didn't do it intentionally, but Marie was Marie. 'What would you like to do? I'm going to scrub floors, polish furniture, clean walls and ceilings — things like that.'

'Ugh! Haven't you got anything better, something creative, for me to do?'

'Like?' Amy pondered. 'You could sort out old towels, bed linen in the cupboards and drawers if you like — check if there's anything worth keeping. I already threw some of it away today. It all smelled a bit; even the curtains went.'

'Ugh! That sounds utterly fascinating, but honestly it's not really my sort of work, is it? What else?'

Amy was running out of ideas. She said weakly, 'You can make the tea!'

Marie was quiet for a moment. 'Curtains? They're coming down?'

Amy nodded at the phone. 'Yes. They're already down; they were old when Aunt Sally lived here, and now they were old, smelly and useless.'

'What about new ones? I'm not bad with a sewing machine. If you buy some material, I could put new ones together, while you're busy playing Mrs Beeton. You do have electricity, I hope?'

Amy didn't need to think twice. Marie was brilliant with a sewing machine. She was pretty helpless at most things, but sewing was something she did well. 'Yes, Ben had it re-connected this week. Making curtains is a wonderful idea! I could go to the market tomorrow morning and get some material.'

'Right that's settled then. Measure from where the curtain rod or rail is, to wherever the end of curtains will be. You need that, plus a narrow top seam, and a wide bottom seam, and then you multiply that three times the width of each window, so that the curtains have folds. We may as well line them. They'll hang better and last longer.

'Don't buy cheap material, I hate messing about with cheap stuff, it doesn't pay in the long run. Go to the stall at the end, and tell him you need good quality stuff. He knows me, so tell him I'll scalp him if it shrinks, changes colour or doesn't wash properly. Get matching cotton, curtain band etc. He'll sort it out for you. His name is Bob, Bill, or was it Barney?'

'You're a gem, Marie! I'll measure the windows, and come for you. OK?'

'Right! Think about what colour scheme you want for these rooms.'

Candidly Amy admitted, 'I'm amazed that you're able to figure things out!'

Marie was affronted. 'I may not be Madame Curie, but I do have five GCEs.'

'And you'd have a lot more if you hadn't spent all your time in the disco instead of revising.'

'Oh, stop preaching! That cottage is beginning to get to you. You're starting to sound more like Aunt Sally every day!'

4

The silence was something she had to get used to. Amy had to admit that she felt nervous. It was a brisk ten minutes walk to the village from the cottage, and her nearest neighbour was across some fields behind the house. During the daytime it was no problem, but when the sun sent long shadows through the garden she recollected how comforting it had been to hear the sounds of other people living in the flat below. She checked the locks and closed the curtains long before the last traces of daylight had faded.

Ben employed a building firm who were good, and knew what they were doing. They got on with the job with no fuss and bother. After a couple of days Amy was able to match names with faces and Bert, the foreman, always had time for a chat when he saw her.

Perhaps her willingness to provide them with tea and biscuits when she was at home helped.

One afternoon she got home earlier than usual. The workmen were still busy when she got home. Her first wish was to change into something more comfortable. The steps creaked as she ran up the simple staircase with its half-landing. Her aunt's narrow thread-bare carpet was still held in place by brass stair-rods in the angle of the steps. Amy hadn't yet decided whether to replace the carpet, or have the staircase completely sanded down and just have a bare wooden surface.

Autumn was already in the air. She looked out of the window at the golden light of the late afternoon lying across the fields adjacent to the house. An ancient apple tree with gnarled, thick bark in the garden was already rapidly losing its leaves. Scrambling into jeans and a midnight-blue turtle-necked sweater, she fought to open the old sash window to let fresh air into her bedroom, the air was cool and sweet and very pure.

Halfway down the stairs, part of the carpeting came away and Amy grabbed the rail tighter although she couldn't stop herself sliding down the last couple of steps on her bottom. It happened so quickly that a few seconds later she was sprawled on the floor in the hallway.

She struggled like an upturned tortoise for a few seconds, and was still struggling when the foreman, who'd heard the commotion, put his head round the door. 'Hey there! What happened to you?'

'I slipped on the stairs, but I'm all right.'

'Sure?' He held out a work-roughened hand to pull her up. 'Certain you're OK?'

Amy appreciated his kindness. Bert was old enough to be her father and his concern brought back memories of how protective her father had been. She nodded. 'I'm certain, just bruising I expect!' She smiled at him reassuringly and walked towards the kitchen.

His voice drifted after her. 'Make

yourself a cup of strong tea with lots of sugar, and sit down for a moment, love. I'll have a look at the stairs.'

She turned and watched him for a moment as he lumbered up the steps of the staircase. One of her elbows was burning. She heard him moving about on the stairs as she made the tea. He joined her in the kitchen and told her he'd found some loose screws. He accepted her invitation to a cup of tea, and Amy listened as he told her about his grandchildren and children.

Ben called just before the men were finishing for the day. He and the foreman discussed the day's progress, talked about possible solutions to problems, and then about generalities. Finally Ben said he'd call on Amy before leaving.

The foreman rubbed his hand across his chin. 'She fell down stairs this afternoon.'

Ben's brows lifted and looked surprised. 'Is she all right?'

'As far as I can judge. She's bruised a

bit, and is probably more shaken than she admits, but she was lucky. She could have broken her neck!'

'What happened? Slipped I suppose?'

'Yes! Oh the stairs — the carpeting came away. She slid down the last couple of steps to the bottom.' The lines of his face intensified.

Ben sensed that something was still left unsaid. 'And?' He watched the older man; Ben's eyebrows raised a fraction.

'Well . . . I checked, and the carpeting is held in place with old-fashioned brass rods — you know the kind, the rods go through a ring attached to the back of the tread.'

Ben nodded. 'Yes.' His expression was in suspense.

'The screws holding one rod on that bit of carpet, was missing completely, and screws on the two steps above that were loose but still holding. I've re-screwed them all, of course.'

Ben's face mirrored his unease. 'Hmm! The house hasn't been lived in for years and wood expands and contracts all the time. Screws or nails won't necessarily hold for ever.'

The foreman nodded. 'Agreed, but it was funny that all the other screws were darkened with age, with the exception of these three steps!'

A silence enveloped them both for a moment.

Ben's expression was sombre. 'Do you mean someone tampered with them?'

'Well . . . ' Bert scratched his head. 'I wouldn't go that far, but it's funny, isn't it? Perhaps the last owner just had them replaced for some reason, and it wasn't done properly.'

Ben's expression was thoughtful. 'Hmm, perhaps.' He stared up at the house and the windows reflecting the afternoon light. 'You're probably right! But let's not jump to conclusions. If you notice anything else out of the ordinary again let me know, will you Bert? It's probably nothing to worry about. I don't want to make Amy nervous with unfounded speculations.'

Bert nodded his agreement. 'Right sir!' He looked at his watch. 'See you Monday morning then, ten-thirty?'

Ben was deep in thought. 'Eh? Oh, yes — yes of course! I'll get on to the building suppliers Monday morning and get the pipes out here first thing. See you Monday, Bert! Have a good weekend!'

Ben made his way towards the small porch. The outer and inner doors were open and some weak sunshine was fighting its way through the narrow window slits on to the stone flagging. He mused that the porch would be a very effective weather break when the new windows and door were fitted. He knocked briefly before he put his head round the corner and called. 'Amy? Ben here! Can I come in?'

Her voice drifted through from the kitchen. 'Of course, I'm in here!'

She was standing at the old-fashioned sink. The soap suds frothed generously over the edge of a plastic bowl as she lifted and rearranged a pullover in its depth. She turned her head briefly to look at him as he came in; she blinked feeling light-headed and the corners of her mouth turned upwards.

His lips twitched slightly, but he said gravely. 'I hear you've turned the staircase into a ski-slope!' The casual tone vanished as he asked. 'Are you all right?'

Her pale cheeks flushed briefly. 'Who told you? Bert I suppose? Nothing to make a fuss about!'

'You haven't answered my question!'

Loose tendrils of hair softened her face, and her hands were hidden beneath a mountain of frothy soap suds. She was acutely conscious of him; he seemed to fill the room. 'Yes, I'm fine. Bruised, but nothing worse than that.'

She found herself swimming through a haze of unknown feelings about this man. He confused her thoughts and she faltered in the brief silence that engulfed them for a moment.

'Good. I just popped in to say hello. I'll be off!'

'Would you like a . . . a cup of coffee?'

He shook his head. His dark hair gleamed in the light. 'Thanks, next time perhaps?'

She nodded silently and her heart thumped erratically as she viewed him.

Ben mused that her smooth skin and arresting, irregular beauty were very special attractions. Her dark blue sweater couldn't hide the suggestion of curves either, and she had a slender body with slim hips. He shook his wandering thoughts, and hoped his tone was casual. 'Bye, Amy! Take care. If you want to live dangerously, do so when in company.'

It was early Saturday morning and it had been a very cold night. Frost still covered the tips of the grass in the neighbouring field with caps of thin ice. The low mist had lifted and was disappearing under the steadily strength-ening sun. Persistent hammering on the door brought Amy rushing downstairs. She was wrapped in a pale blue fleecy dressing gown, fair-isle bobble-cap in shades of beige and lilac, and a pair of thick ankle socks.

Ben did nothing to hide his amusement when she opened the door. He spluttered and his laugh came out deep and strong. His dark-brown eyes were full of merriment. 'Good morning! Amy? It is Amy . . . ?'

She snatched the woolly cap from her head, but it didn't improve appearances much as, unknown to herself, her hair now stood on end, and she looked more peculiar than ever. She went bright pink with embarrassment and when she spoke her voice was belligerent. 'What do you want?'

Although he tried not to, he finally gave in and threw back his head before he let out another peal of laughter. He smothered his amusement long enough to say. 'Is it some kind of new fashion? Or do you usually dress like that on Saturdays?'

Amy flushed. 'For your information, it was very cold last night — and I had

54

to keep myself warm somehow!'

He gave another belly laugh. 'You wore that in bed? Why not get an electric blanket?'

Amy mused briefly that those dark eyes and wicked grin turned him into a real life hero. She shook her thoughts and tried to compose herself. 'It's not worth the expenditure; I'm hoping to have central heating soon! I don't care what I look like, as long as I'm warm.'

Trying to look unconcerned while feeling a war of emotions raging within her, she crossed her arms in a defensive gesture and tried to normalise the conversation. 'Does your unexpected Saturday morning visit have a special reason, or did you just come to annoy me?'

'I came to warn you; they're coming to install the heating on Monday.'

Her eyes brightened considerably and she gave up all attempts at detachment. 'Really? That's the best news I've heard for weeks.'

Ben felt just as pleased as she looked.

'This company is usually very good about not making too much mess, but I don't know if they'll go wild when they work in the middle of all this.' His hand gestured around. 'They may throw all attempts at keeping things tidy to the wind, thinking that you won't notice a bit more dirt.'

'That would be understandable.' She drew the dressing gown closer to her body. 'Like to come in? A cup of coffee?'

'I thought you'd never ask!'

Heading for the stairs, she said. 'Be with you in a minute! I'll just change into something more suitable.'

He smiled at her departing figure and nodded. 'I'll make the coffee.'

She shouted over her shoulder as she went up the stairs two at a time. 'Coffee and filter in the cupboard next to the window, mugs are on the draining board, milk is in the fridge!'

Amy dressed quickly in jeans and a thick cable sweater, and forced a brush through her tangled hair. No time for make-up, but the reflection in the mirror was a decided improvement. Her slippers clattered on the stairs as she hurried back to the kitchen.

The kettle was boiling. He'd already turned on the electric fire in the corner, and it had taken the edge off the chill in the room. She sat down, accepted a mug of steaming coffee from his outstretched hand, circling it with her hands gratefully. 'I don't usually sleep as long as this. I took a long time to fall asleep because it was so cold last night and then I overslept this morning.'

His eyes swept over her face approvingly as he sipped his coffee. 'No need to explain. I'm not judging you.' There was a moment's silence; then he said. 'If you want to know the truth, I think you've coped great so far.' Bereft of make-up, her face looked very soft and finely textured.

Amy blushed a pale pink, more pleased than she cared to admit to hear those words from his lips. 'Can I do anything to speed things up for

Monday? Move furniture out of the way, or roll up the carpets?'

He stretched his arm across the neighbouring empty seat gripping the back, and his brown eyes were unblinking. 'Good heavens, no! Leave everything where it is. They know that the main heating unit goes into the former outhouse, and they know where to put the radiators from my plans. It's up to them how they do it.'

He played with the handle of the mug and regarded her carefully for a moment. He wore a checked shirt under a classical navy pullover and smart grey trousers. Amy wished she could stop studying him in such detail. It was as if she were addicted to him.

He leaned forward. 'You know that you chose the wrong time of year to do this, don't you?'

She nodded. 'Perhaps I should have waited until the heating was in, but I just think about the rent I've saved. Once the place is heated I'll be inspired to do some decorating. Even if there weren't ditches, I won't be able to do much outside in the garden until spring anyway.'

It was very quiet, and sunlight was beginning to find its way through the windows. One of his hands was resting on the checked fringed tablecloth; it was tanned with long fingers and neat nails. She jumped when she heard him ask.

'Do you like gardening?'

'I don't know — this is the first garden I've ever had. I'm going to get some books from the library and read up about the basic things during the winter.'

She sighed softly. 'Who knows, I might actually like pottering about in the garden.'

'Umm! No good asking me for advice or encouragement. I haven't a clue about that sort of thing; my flat has a tiny balcony and the space behind the office is just an area of cement slabs. By the way, I'll tell them to put a temporary hot water tap in the kitchen, so that you've a constant supply of hot water!'

'Oh, yes please! That would be wonderful. Just the thought of constant hot water . . . I could kiss you for that.' She spoke without thinking.

'Be my guest!'

His smile softened his features and sent shivers down her spine. A warning voice told her to appear unconcerned. She felt disorientated by her reactions but she looked straight at him and smiled. 'Thanks, Ben! I must be a big headache at times, I seem to be harping on about something every time you call.'

He shrugged his shoulders. 'True! But it's my job. I'm used to it; people are impatient, sub-contractors don't keep to schedule, suppliers mess things up, and I'm there to sort it out.' His voice was serious, but Amy saw the unmistakable flash of amusement in his eyes. 'I must admit that seeing you first thing in the morning in a bobble cap has made every single complaint worthwhile, but I don't know if I could face it again!'

Amy grabbed a potholder from the table and threw it at his head. 'You're clearly a coward!'

Ben caught it in mid-air while ducking and he laughed. He looked at his watch. 'I wish I'd had a camera with me — I could have blackmailed you for the rest of your life. Well, I'll be off. Oh, my mother said she was going to call. Has she been?'

'Your mother? No, not as far as I know. Any special reason?'

'Oh, you know — the usual thing. You're new in the village, and I mentioned your name, told her who you were, etc., etc. I think she's curious to see what you're like. In other words she's just being plain nosy.'

'What's her name?'

'Marjorie. And Dad is called Peter. He works as a management consultant, and Mum gave up work years ago, because living in the village made travelling to her job such a drag.'

'Marjorie? Aunt Sally mentioned her several times — she visited my aunt now and then, didn't she?'

Ben shrugged his shoulder. 'Perhaps — I don't really know.'

'If she found time to visit Aunt Sally, she must be a nice person.'

Ben grinned. 'You women do stick together, don't you? Anyway I hope the heating company arrives before you leave. If not, you'll have to leave the door open. I can't get here before 9.30.'

He took a business card out of his wallet. 'But my private number — I don't think you have that. The other is my office number and it switches automatically to my flat if no-one answers.'

She took the small rectangular bit of paper. 'Will they finish the work on Monday?'

The smile that lit his eyes was one of pure amusement, and he shook his head. 'Not likely! If you're lucky they'll be through it all by Wednesday.'

'Know anyone to help you move the

heavy stuff like the washing machine?'
He studied how her brown hair clustered in short curls around her face.

She answered quickly. 'Mike — he's a gem!'

He hesitated for a moment lost in thought, and then he got up, put his mug in the sink and turned. 'Good! I'll be in touch.'

Amy nodded and saw him off. She closed the door and leaned against it. She shook herself, and told herself she'd plenty to do, she didn't have time to daydream about Ben Tyler.

5

It was warm and cosy in the cottage. The heating company hadn't made too much mess. Downstairs they'd moved furniture to install the radiators and pipes, and put it all back afterwards.

The following Saturday afternoon she was busy clearing up some of the worst of the mess along the outer borders of the garden. It was a bright September day full of sunshine. Somewhere in the hedge a bird was singing and the breezes played with the remaining leaves on the trees. She knew it was almost pointless to do any gardening until the ditches had been filled in, but she felt a need to tidy and improve appearances as much as she could. She'd already attacked the ancient ivy that criss-crossed the stonework of the outhouse.

She needed a ladder to cut away at

the strands high up on the wall — where it was already climbing over the trough on to the roof.

She looked up briefly as she noticed someone walking along the road, and returned to her work. Amy was surprised when the woman stopped at her gate.

She said. 'Hello, you must be Amy.'

'Yes.' Amy didn't recognise her, and was puzzled.

'I'm Marjorie Tyler. Ben is helping you to get this lovely old place back into shape, isn't he?'

'Mrs Tyler?' She hurried to remove her gardening gloves, and thrust out her hand. 'How kind of you to call. Everything is still a mess, but one day I hope it'll look as tidy as it was when Aunt Sally lived here.'

The older woman smiled and shook her hand. 'I'm sure! The cottage used to be such a picturesque place. I'm so glad that someone has moved in again. Ben told me about you. He said I'd be a busybody if I called, but I think calling on a newcomer is part of village life.' Her blue eyes twinkled and her cheeks bulged slightly as she gave Amy a warm smile.

Amy liked her on sight. She had a motherly smile. She was mid-height, with bright blue eyes and dark brown hair.

Amy stuffed her gloves into the bib pocket. 'It takes a special kind of courage to visit strangers — Ben's talking nonsense! You're the first person from the village I've met properly. Would you like a cup of tea?'

'That would be lovely, but I don't want to interrupt you.' She looked around. 'You're clearly very busy.' She lifted a dish covered in silver foil. 'I've brought you a blackberry tart. I was making one for us for tomorrow, and I thought you might like one too.'

'That is kind! To be honest I'm glad to have an excuse to stop. I can't really do much in the garden apart from tidying, until the ditches are filled! I'm just quieting my conscience. I won't be

66

able to do any serious work until springtime.'

Marjorie Tyler looked around with interest and then at Amy. 'They've certainly made a mess of the garden, haven't they? It looks like an archaeological dig! Sally wouldn't have liked it one bit. You need a torch to get around at night, I expect?'

'I do! Even to go to the toilet! At least the pathway is still fairly intact in places but I try to avoid walking around outside after dark if I can. Let's go in, my mouth is already watering at the thought of a piece of tart!'

Marjorie looked around the hall. 'It's lovely to see life in these rooms again. This is such a cosy little cottage, isn't it? The living-room is a good size and the view from the windows across the fields is really pretty. Some modern houses aren't as big as this, and they're often not as solid either. The kitchen is small, but it was big enough for your aunt. She managed very well, until she had difficulty walking — she hated being dependent on other people.'

'Ben suggested that we integrated the outhouse, and put the central heating, washing machine, freezer, etc. in there. Now I have plenty of room.'

'What a good idea!'

'Come and have a look!'

Marjorie Tyler approved vocally and Amy began to make them tea. Marjorie went back to the living-room. She was standing looking out of the windows towards the neighbour farm when Amy came in. 'I was just thinking how pleased your aunt would be to know you're living here. Planning to change much more?'

Amy brushed her hair back behind her ears with her hand. 'No, I don't think so, apart from making a bathroom out of the smallest bedroom and a downstairs toilet in the hall. Ben is trying to keep as much of the original structure as he can. He's good at his job, and clever.'

'Umm! So I'm told. He was always interested in buildings, in viaducts, in bridges and things like that. We thought he'd end up as an engineer, but I suppose architects are engineers in a way, aren't they?' She leaned back and smiled. 'Don't tell him I said that — he'll say I'm going senile, give me a lecture on the differences, and buy me a book to illustrate what he's talking about.'

Amy grinned. 'I can imagine! Do you have any other children, Mrs Tyler?'

'No, but please call me Marjorie, Mrs Tyler makes me feel like the village headmistress! I lost a couple of babies before Ben was born, and couldn't have any more after him.' She shrugged. 'I always wanted a big family, but I'm grateful for Ben. What about you? What about your mother and father, do they mind about you coming to live here?' She sipped her tea and leaned back.

'No, I'm the only one. My mother understands why I decided to keep the cottage but she worries about me living here alone. My father died about four years ago. Mum works in a flower shop and seems to have adjusted. They were married for nearly thirty years and they had a happy marriage. It took her a long time to get over his death.'

'Oh dear! I'm sorry — yes, now you mention it, I remember Sal telling me. She was very upset at the time too; your aunt was extremely fond of him, wasn't she?'

Amy nodded in agreement, took a mouthful of the tart; the blackberries with their distinctive fruity taste were delicious. Amy brushed the corner of her mouth with her finger to remove any crumbs. 'Umm! This is just wonderful! Aunt Sally was lovely.'

'I understand why your mother might worry. The cottage is a little off the beaten track, but things are quiet around here. Thank heavens the negative influences of modern society haven't reached us yet. I expect you'll get married. Are you engaged; perhaps you have a boyfriend or a partner?'

'No.' Amy didn't comment any further. It wasn't worth saying that finding someone to love was like chasing a will-o-the-wisp.

Marjorie Tyler looked at her speculatively and gave her a warm smile. 'Another single! I keep hoping Ben will get married. He did have one particular girlfriend for quite a while, but she cheated on him and when he found out I think it made him very cynical.'

Amy would have liked to hear more details about Ben's life, but she resisted the temptation to ask. Ben was her architect; nothing more.

Marjorie looked out of the window overlooking their fields. 'Met Elsie Booth yet? From the farm over there? You can just see the big barn and the farmhouse from here.'

'Yes. She came over when I moved in, with a pot of vegetable broth. It was just what my helpers and I needed. It was very kind of her. I've only had a quick chat with her — when I took the pot back, but I hope we'll get to know each other better. Today you called with your tart; I think I'm going to like the village!' Amy smiled warmly at her visitor.

★ ★ ★

'Oh, please come, Amy. It's my first real part.' Marie's voice was pleading. 'I've got my share of free tickets; it won't cost you anything.'

Amy tried to get out of it. 'There's so much work waiting to be done! With the central heating working, I can start to redecorate the bedrooms. I'm going to start on the middle bedroom and then the guest room when that's finished.'

'Can't you forget about that blasted cottage for one single evening?'

'It is not a blasted cottage, it's my home!'

Marie pleaded. 'Oh, do come! A break will do you good. Ben said so.'

'Did he?' Any wondered when Ben and Marie had been talking about her, but she didn't ask. 'Oh, all right! Anything for peace! When is it?'

'Friday evening, and drinks at the party

72

afterwards for friends. It's the premiere, so we'll all be putting everything into it. Our new producer/director is a pain, but he knows his job.'

'What happened to Potter, Phillips, or whatever his name was? I always felt sorry for the poor man; you had wrapped him firmly round your finger, didn't you?'

Marie wrinkled her nose. 'He got an offer to run a well-known repertory company in Leeds, so he dumped us. He left us to the mercies of this new chap. He's good at his job but I don't like him much. In fact, I can't stand him.'

Amy tilted her head to the side. 'Why? Is he a devoted husband, guarded by a loving fianceé, or is he just immune to your charms? What does he look like?'

'He's single, and good-looking . . . if you like cave-men types, that is.'

'And . . . where's the problem?'

'He's rude, he's demanding, and he can't be manipulated.'

Amy burst out laughing. 'Really? He must be interesting if he can resist you.'

Marie tossed her head defiantly. 'I won't try any more! I've decided to ignore him — off stage. We don't hit it off. He's good at his job; I have to admit that — so we have an unspoken agreement. We work, and avoid each other socially.'

Amy couldn't help it and spluttered — the sound turned into a gurgling laugh. 'Marie! This is wonderful! It's the first time I remember you admitting defeat!'

Marie's voice blazed. 'I am not admitting defeat! I just do not want anything to do with an ignorant, conceited, arrogant macho man, that's all.' In her anger she rushed on without thinking to say, 'Anyone who asks Judy Renshaw out for a drink when I'm around has to be lacking in brains.'

Amy laughed again. 'He asked Judy out? And hasn't asked you? This gets better and better! I'd like to meet the man!'

Amy was acutely aware of Ben sitting at her side as they sat in the darkness. She tried to concentrate on the stage. Marie acted well and was decidedly one of the best performers. In the interval they went to the makeshift bar in the foyer.

After getting them something to drink they moved a little to the side away from the throng. She'd taken trouble with her make up and she looked as good as she felt. She didn't miss Ben's obvious look of approval when he'd divested her of her coat at the cloakroom and was glad she'd made a special effort to look nice.

'She's talented, isn't she?' His voice was interested and relaxed.

The white wine was chilled and had a pleasing fruity undertone. Amy took a sip. 'Yes. I think she's picked the right profession this time.'

Ben took a generous gulp of ginger ale and looked curious. 'This time? What else has she done?'

'Oh . . . Lots of things!'

'Like?'

Amy could only surmise why he was so interested — he was probably already more than just attracted to Marie. Amy didn't want to dwell on that thought for long, so she said hurriedly, 'Well she worked in a boutique for a while, until she started being honest with customers when they asked her if something looked good or not! Some people really wanted the truth; others just wanted her to tell them what they longed to hear. Marie never got the hang of sorting the one from the other, so conflict was inevitable!'

His mouth turned up at the corner. 'I bet!'

'She worked in a veterinary practice for a short time, but soon found that although she loves animals, she hated having to cope with their illnesses and injuries.

'She had a spell as a tourist guide in London, but as she didn't come from London and didn't bother to learn enough about its history, she soon discovered a lot of the visitors knew more than she did anyway, so she gave that up before she was fired. She did some modelling and quite enjoyed that, until she refused to go on a modelling job in the Swiss Alps — because she hates the cold. Then, she . . . '

He held up his hand in protest. 'Please. I get the gist; but somehow it fits, doesn't it? How long has she been acting?'

Amy reckoned quickly. 'About six months now, and I really think she's found something that fits this time. She enjoys it very much, and a lot of the other stage people are just as impetuous, colourful, and unpredictable, so she feels quite at home.'

He laughed softly. 'Yes, there's never a dull moment when she's around, is there. I must say though, she's an excellent actress; she's good at it. What about you? Have you always worked in an office?'

'More or less. I worked for an

accounting company after I left secretarial college, then in the administration of another firm for a couple of years. That's where I met my present boss, and when he started up his business a couple of years ago, he asked me to go with him, so I did!'

He smiled and Amy's pulse quickened.

Amy coloured and felt a moment of sheer pleasure.

6

After the play, Amy and Ben waited in the emptying foyer for Marie to join them. Someone who Amy knew was clearing the glasses and stopped to talk to her for a couple of minutes.

When Marie arrived, Amy and Ben both showered her with praise. Preening with pleasure Marie tucked her arm through Amy's and they joined the rest of the cast, in the nearby pub. There were more people than space, and the cavern-like room vibrated to the sound of music.

Amy didn't want to conjecture whether Marie and Ben had a relationship going, but she couldn't help noticing they got on well and laughed a lot. Marie was being nice to him, and that was always a very meaningful sign. Amy didn't want to wrestle with the knowledge that Ben Tyler had a private life that had nothing to do with her.

She chatted to other company players she knew, and everyone was in high spirits. She found herself opposite a new face.

He asked in a friendly voice, 'Hi! Who are you? You're a fresh face — you're . . . ?'

Amy studied his features, and guessed this must be the new producer. Amy knew most of the others — she'd met them before when Marie had taken her along to other parties. 'Hello! I'm Amy, Marie's cousin.'

'Ah . . . ' His black eyes twinkled cautiously. 'I'm Henry, the producer. What did you think of the play? You can be honest with me; a few well-meant words of criticism are worth a hundred words of praise.'

He was extremely dark like a Spanish gypsy. His face was angular with a hungry look and the shadow of his beard gave him an even manlier aura. He threaded his fingers through a swath of wavy black hair and it promptly flopped back on to his brow; he waited expectantly for her reply.

Marie didn't get on with this man, and Amy was curious enough to find out why. He was attractive and seemed to be very pleasant. 'I honestly enjoyed it.' She stalled him with a raised hand before he could ask. 'I don't know why; I just did. Marie wants analysis from me all the time too, but I keep telling her that I simply like something or not, I don't like evaluating.'

He nodded understandingly and smiled.

Amy paused a moment. 'Marie did well tonight, didn't she?'

He answered casually. 'Marie? Yes she gave a good performance.' He eyed her speculatively. 'If she was more disciplined, more professional, she could go right to the top. She's talented and puts everything into her acting, but that isn't enough. A good actor also has to accept constructive criticism, and take well-meant advice.'

'You mean that she doesn't? Is she rebelling, being egotistical?'

He gave her a crooked smile. 'Egoistical is too strong perhaps. She seems to care passionately about acting, but she is very self-centred, and she's often insensitive to the aims and needs of the company as a whole.'

Amy took a sip of orange juice and savoured the sweetly sharp taste on her tongue. She dug deeper. 'In what way? Is she late for rehearsals; fluffs her lines — that sort of thing?'

He had a reflective look on his face; he was probably wondering how honest he could be. 'No, but she's hard to control and knows everything better.' He paused a second. 'I don't like talking about her behind her back, but if you are her cousin, someone who knew her well, I think there's nothing wrong with me admitting that some-times I'm at a loss as how to handle her. How close are you and Marie? Can you influence her?'

Taken slightly aback she said, 'We're close because we're related, but we are good friends too. I know she can be difficult to handle, but that's her temperament; I don't think she's intentionally insensitive. Sometimes I think she's covering up her insecurity.'

About to gulp some beer from his glass, he spluttered and laughed loudly. 'Insecure? She's as insecure as a horned viper!'

Amy caught sight of Ben. One of the other actresses had him in her clutches; his expression was uptight. Amy also saw Marie, talking to someone on the other side of the room — a gregarious lighting technician who thought he was God's gift to women. Amy wondered if that was the reason why Ben was looking so serious.

She turned her attention to Henry again. 'No, honestly! Her parents ran a dancing school, and she didn't have a very secure childhood. They were always busy with competitions and events; it left them very little time for Marie. She was dumped with relatives and strangers all the time, and I think that made her resentful and turned her

83

into a bit of a rebel.

'Marie tends to think that if you disagree with her, you are in opposition just to annoy her; I'm sure if you explained why you want something done in a certain way, she'd knuckle under. She loves acting. She needs to understand exactly what you expect, and why.'

She was certain Marie would kill her if she could hear her. Amy was also sure Marie's antipathy for this man was unfounded — he was a perfectly normal person. There was nothing to suggest that he was unreasonable, so she ploughed on. 'Perhaps it isn't all her fault? You seem to knock sparks off each other; it's not strange when your lines of communication get crossed all the time, is it?'

His lips parted in surprise. 'Did she tell you that?'

'That you don't get on? Yes! And I must say I was surprised. Marie gets on with nearly everyone. She's impulsive, and she likes having her own way, but she loves acting more than anything and she'd be devastated if you sacked her.' Her green eyes studied him and emphasised her pleading tone. 'Couldn't you just accept her as she is, and ignore her faults?'

He rubbed his chin. 'I can't afford to 'accept' her as you put it, and I can't afford to ignore the way she wants to oppose me all the time either. Even if I had the time to pander to her whims, which I don't, my job is to form the cast into a functioning machine. She's just one member of the cast.'

'If you don't mind me saying so, it sounds like you both need to take a small step forward.' Amy took a deep breath; it was none of her business. 'I know that she respects you profession-ally, so the difficulties must be on a more personal level. Why not talk to her? I'm sure if you explain what you expect from an actress, and why, that she'll understand. I'll have a word with her, and soften her up a bit if you like.'

He laughed quietly and his smile

echoed in his voice. 'I wonder if she knows how lucky she is to have a champion like you?'

Someone grabbed him by the arm and dragged him away. He lifted his hand in farewell and gave her an irresistible grin.

A voice drifted over her shoulder. 'Amy! Have you had enough of all this by any chance?' His deep voice broke into her reveries.

She turned to face him. 'Oh, Ben! Yes! Yes, I think I have. Why? Do you want to go?'

Ben surveyed them silently, and something flickered in his eyes. 'All this chitchat and small talk about acting isn't really my thing. This room is enough to make me permanently claustrophobic.'

She looked round at the murky room and listened to the general loud hubbub and noisy music. She said firmly, 'You're right! We can go whenever we like. Look, you don't have to take me home either! I can get a taxi. I warned you, when you suggested picking me up, that it would tie you down. Driving me home will only take you out of your way. I could have come with my own car.'

'Nonsense!' He took her elbow and guided her gently towards where their coats were buried beneath a myriad of others.

Amy tried to get into the low-slung sports car elegantly but had to grab the doorframe as she misjudged the amount of space she had. She sighed inwardly in frustration; unaware that Ben grinned in the driver's seat as he wondered if she'd land in his lap. Amy was glad to be finally settled, even though Ben's nearness disturbed her, and she felt nervous.

She mused that by now she'd held lots of conversations with Ben, and still had a feeling of bewilderment and conflicting emotions when they were alone together.

The headlights cut like a knife through the darkness on the journey back to the cottage. Neither of them said much on the way. Amy couldn't think spontaneously of any common theme apart from the house, the play or Marie and she didn't want to mention any of those.

They turned the corner at the top of the lane and Amy bent to pick up the shoulder bag at her feet. As he glanced towards the house, Ben thought he saw a light moving near one of the corners. The hedge was a barrier of intertwined bare twigs from close up, but from a distance its winter framework provided a fairly clear view of what was beyond.

There was a speck of light for a moment, and then it disappeared again. Ben wasn't really sure if he'd seen anything at all, so he didn't mention it. Amy wasn't aware of what he thought he'd seen; she was busy hoisting her bag to her shoulder. She got out when he drew up outside the gate. A little further down the lane Ben saw red tail-lights of a car, and heard an engine surge to life.

Amy was still deciding whether it would look as if she was hoping for more than friendship if she asked him in for a nightcap?

Ben eliminated any necessity for further thought; he leaned forward across her and opened the door swiftly. He didn't even bother to get out of the car as he said, 'Good night, Amy! Don't forget to lock the doors. I'll be in touch at the beginning of the week.'

Amy flushed in the shadows, glad that he couldn't see her face. Having done his duty, he was now very anxious to get away. She got out, lifted her hand in thanks while turning away from him, and pushed open the squeaking gate. His car roared off in the direction of the village. Amy looked up at the sky briefly, and took a deep breath of the cold night air.

She tried not to think about Ben, and studied the skeleton outlines of the dark trees huddled behind the hedge at the back of the cottage. At the porch Amy fumbled around in her bag for the key, and once she was inside she locked up and climbed upstairs with a bleak expression.

Just a few miles away, Ben realised he'd lost track of the mysterious car, and he hit the steering wheel with the palm of his hand in frustration.

★   ★   ★

The electrical company was busy rewiring; and Amy knew they were trying to keep the dirt and dust to a minimum.

Ben was talking to the electrician when she got home one afternoon. After a while he joined her in the kitchen. Her own modern cooker was integrated into the working section of the kitchen, near to Aunt Sally's old-fashioned sink. Bert had helped her put up her kitchen cupboards, and now that the larger appliances were next door in the new utility room she had plenty of space to stand Aunt Sally's Welsh dresser against the wall.

Ben's eyes followed her as she made them coffee; they were intent and appraising. He ran his hands through his crisp black hair. 'Are you satisfied with this electrician?'

She looked up from filling the kettle and there was fresh high colour in her face. 'Yes. In fact, he's very obliging and he's made some good suggestions.'

Amy handed him a mug of steaming coffee, and walked ahead of him into the living room with hers cupped in her hands. He followed. She took a deep breath and tried to relax. It was hard to understand why she felt tense whenever Ben was around.

He made himself comfortable in one of the easy chairs alongside the Victorian grate with its panels of decorative side tiling. It had a cast-iron hood, and a solid black fire basket. It used to be Aunt Sally's main source of heating. Now it was no longer necessary for that but Amy intended to keep it; she thought it was an attractive eye-catcher. Clearly, Ben agreed.

She was curious. 'To be honest I thought you wouldn't commend unpractical things like cast-iron grates. I thought architects were mad about modern buildings and funky facilities.'

He pondered her remark for a second. 'Good heavens, no! Perhaps some famous architects get reputations and lots of praise for special projects, but the majority of us move in completely different spheres. Every generation of architects produces what's needed, and usually lots of good and practical things develop. You can follow the progress of civilisation by just studying the path of development from Stone Age dwellings to today's skyscrapers.'

'You like your work don't you?'

He spoke with the certainty of someone who wasn't just a dreamer. 'Of course, I wouldn't do it otherwise. A lot of architects design furniture and all sorts of other things these days, as well as buildings. Have you ever heard of Corbusier?'

Amy searched her mind; the name

rang a bell. 'Was he the one who designed furniture? If he's the right one, I've seen pictures of a super divan — very modern and uncluttered, made out of leather and polished steel. I think it's a sought-after classic item nowadays.'

Ben looked at her approvingly. 'You're right, he designed some fantastic buildings but he also made comfortable, modern and practical furniture. Sometimes he created prestige things like churches and private homes; sometimes he did living complexes for working class people. He designed with people in mind, not necessarily just for money, although he made plenty of that in the course of his life.'

She fidgeted with her mug, and noticed him studying her face.

He stuck his long legs out in a straight line and leaned back; his hands cupped protectively around his mug. With amusement in his voice he changed direction and asked, 'What about the ghost? Any recent sightings?'

Amy was silent, looked down at the pattern on the red and blue Turkish carpet and then met his eye again.

He chuckled. 'Amy! Don't tell me . . . you've actually seen the ghost?'

Her sense of humour bubbled over and she had difficulty in suppressing an urge to giggle. 'Well, I can't be sure, but I think . . . think, mind you . . . that I saw something glowing or luminous, in the garden the other evening. I was frightened to death at the time, and just shut the curtains. I didn't have enough courage to look again. It was probably only a figment of my imagination — a reflection of something in the moon-light — but in a place like this, and after what you said . . . '

His smile vanished, and was replaced by an expression of surprise. He stiff-ened. 'When did this happen?'

Amy reached up to play with her hair. It seemed ridiculous even to mention it now; in a jesting tone she said. 'Sunday evening. It was already pitch-dark, about half-past nine, I think.'

He said smoothly without expression, 'Could you see anything in detail?'

Amy looked at him in surprise. He sounded serious. She'd thought he'd make fun. 'Nothing I can describe, you know how many ditches and piles of earth there are out there, but the sky was clear and the moon was bright. Oh, forget it, Ben! It was just a fleeting impression. Living on my own makes me jumpy. A psychologist would probably tell me, I saw what I expected to see.'

He shrugged, and leaned forward to put his mug on a side-table. 'Is it a problem for you? Living here on your own?'

Amy avoided his eyes and glanced towards the window. The sky was laden with grey clouds and it was raining heavily. 'I'm getting used to it; I'm not as nervous as I was.'

'But it's still a problem? Tell you what . . . I'll get in touch with a security company at the beginning of the week. We'll ask them for an estimate on how much it will cost to increase the safety factor of the cottage.'

'It'll be expensive!'

'Do you want peace of mind, or not? The cottage is solidly built. If you had alarms on the windows, and a coded lock on the door you'll feel a lot safer. I can still tell the window people to put in a coded panel in the door and safety locks on the windows, it's still not too late for that.' He was silent for a moment. 'An additional alarm system that automatically connects to the local police or a security company will only cost a small amount every month — and I'll guarantee you'll feel a lot safer.'

Amy was surprised how serious he was taking her remarks. 'I may be scared but no-one is going to chase me out of the cottage. Ghost or no ghost, I'm here to stay, but go ahead and find out how much it will cost, if you think I can still afford it!'

7

The air was full of the smell of earth after rain, and mud clung to her Wellingtons in heavy lumps. Amy stood contemplating the garden; thinking about how to plan for the future. They were using an excavator at the moment, filling in the ditches and levelling out the surface. Amy decided to ask Ben if the driver would level out the old rockery at the back of the cottage while he was at it.

Amy had noticed the sunlight lingered there in the afternoon; it would be the perfect spot to put a patio. It was hidden from the road by the cottage and sheltered from the wind by the hedge and the trees.

On impulse she went back to the house, shook off her Wellingtons in the porch and rang Ben's number. She knew the number for his office and his flat was the same, so she wasn't surprised that it rang several times and then there was an audible click before someone answered. Her breath caught in her throat when it was a female voice. It also wasn't Marie's voice either.

'Hello! Julie Watson speaking!'

Amy gathered her shattered ease and spoke a little breathlessly. 'Oh, hello! I . . . I wanted to talk to Ben if possible, please.'

'Ben isn't here at the moment. Can I take a message.'

'No, it's not that important. I can talk to him another time.'

The voice sounded restless. 'Well . . . if you're sure?' There was the sound of a kettle whistling in the background. 'He said he might be out for awhile, and that usually means he'll be late. Perhaps you'd like to ring back later?'

Amy took a deep breath; the woman seemed to know all about him and his movements. 'No, please it's all right. I'll call him tomorrow.' The whistle shrilled on. 'Thanks! Goodbye!'

Amy put down the phone quickly, bit her lip in dismay and swallowed a lump in her throat. Somehow Amy was really glad she hadn't mentioned her name.

The following weekend, Marie came for a sudden visit on Saturday afternoon. She made a quick inspection of the rooms while Amy peeled some apples for them to nibble. Marie flopped into one of the large fireside chairs, and drew up a leg to tuck it neatly under her body. She reached forward, took a thick slice of apple, bit into the juicy flesh, and started to talk with her mouth half-full.

'Well ... there's an all round improvement on last time, but still an awful lot to do, isn't there? The rooms look like you moved in yesterday and still haven't unpacked most of the boxes. There's a thick layer of dust on your curtains already; you'll have to wash them when the workers have finished. You should have waited to put them up!'

'I know! Ben warned me it would be

a waste of time to do much decorating until they've finished the central heating, the wiring, the plumbing, and fixing the doors and windows, but I was tempted by the picture of at least having the windows look decent. Luckily they are all washable and good quality, thanks to you, so apart from having to iron them, I don't think that it'll be much of a problem. At the moment, the main problem is keeping pace with the dust and the dirt.'

Marie picked up a glass of orange juice. 'Ugh! That sounds fun! How far are things?'

'The central heating is finished, the wiring is more or less complete, the windows and doors are supposed to arrive in a couple of weeks, and the plumber has started to turn the smallest bedroom into a bathroom. They've already partitioned off part of the hall.'

Marie studied her glossy nails, and put her empty glass on the nearby table. 'I must say I think you're managing great amid all this havoc. I'd go bonkers! And I'd probably murder any man in blue dungarees who came within two miles of the front door! In fact you also happen to have plenty of open ditches out there to dispose of bodies at the moment, don't you? If there is a competition for the yuckiest building site of the year, you'd win!'

Amy grinned and laughed out loud. Marie was a tonic. 'Yes! I agree! But wait until this time next year, it will all look wonderful and you'll envy me then. Luckily I'm not around when the dust flies; I find it spread evenly over everything when I get home. I do admit that I'm fed up with cleaning but I keep telling myself it will end, eventually. I'll need a new vacuum if it goes on much longer.'

'Rather you than me! The mere thought of non-stop cleaning is enough to give me permanent nightmares, and send me storming off the nearest cliff like a lemming.'

Amy nodded and smiled. 'I know!' Amy leaned back enjoying the chance to gossip for a change. 'I haven't seen you for ages. How are things? The play is doing well, isn't it? In last week's issue, the newspaper mentioned it was sold out for the next couple of weeks. The article even mentioned your name. Did you see it?'

Marie's chin lifted a centimetre and her eyes sparkled. 'Yes, of course. The first time in print! For once there was something sensible in the rag and not just the usual kind of articles about church bazaars, radar traps and lost grannies. I can feel how the audience is sometimes really caught up in the plot; I have them in the palm of my hand! This is what I was born to do!'

Amy moved a cushion casually to one side, and patted it. 'That's good! What about Henry? Any improvement? Have you thought about what I told you?'

Marie's colour heightened. 'Well . . . since we talked together, he and I agreed on a truce. He's still the world's greatest male egotist, and completely overbearing into the bargain . . . but he's a fantastic producer!' She shifted in her seat. 'He and I talked things through one evening over a drink, and I decided to give him a break, as long as he treats me fair.'

Amy was amused. 'Really?' She put as much innocent surprise into her voice as she could. 'Did you agree to give him a chance, or did he say he'd give you one?'

Marie's fingers fidgeted with the glass. 'Let's just say we met half-way! We've agreed on a ceasefire in the active battleground of the theatre!' Her hand made a vague movement, and then she pounced on another chunk of apple. She nibbled a bit and continued. 'I must say even though I can't stand him . . . ' She bit off another crisp mouthful and paused. ' . . . the suggestions he makes about my role are spot on. I can tell by the way the audience react.'

Amy tilted her head to one side. 'I talked to him that evening I came to see you in the play. He seemed a perfectly nice chap to me.'

'Amy, mass murderers act like normal people most of the time! Anyone can appear to be nice, if they want to, even Henry Lawson. Your misguided belief that men are humans leads you astray all the time, doesn't it? It's probably why you pick such hopeless boyfriends. It's about time you started searching seriously, before all the best ones have disappeared from the shelves. If you're not careful you'll end up as prime candidate for the spinster of the century!'

Amy felt piqued with Marie; it didn't happen often, but she felt very tempted to give her a mouthful. 'Why don't you just live your life your way; and leave me to mine? I'm happy as I am. You may be surprised to know that life does have interests other than running after men!'

Marie opened her eyes wide, surprised at Amy's outbreak. 'Hey! No offence intended, love; I'm not trying to annoy you. I just want to point out that you can't live without love, Amy!'

Amy changed the subject hurriedly. 'What's wrong with Henry exactly? He's a very attractive bohemian character. He's friendly, polite, intelligent, and you just admitted that he knows his job.'

Marie blinked. 'Wrong? It's obvious! He lays the law down too much. He's despotic like his namesake, Henry VIII.'

'Oh, don't be silly! Your Henry is responsible for what he says and does — to the people who own the theatre. Henry VIII was a law unto himself. You were against Henry from the start. And I suspect it's because he doesn't jump through your hoop like all the rest do!'

Marie studied her nails closely. 'I'm really not interested in Mr Wonderful. I have other fish to fry. I'd have to be pretty desperate to want 'know it all better, Henry Lawson'.'

Amy decided to ignore dirt for once, and any thoughts about decorating or gardening, and go to church the following Sunday morning. Ben's mother had come up to the cottage to welcome her to the village, and the church was a logical launching pad for joining in with local activities.

Later on, when she wasn't constantly up to her eyes in work, she looked forward to being part of village activities. She'd noticed several posters hung in the village shop inviting people to join the local dramatic society held in the community hall, and then there was a list of evening classes at the local school.

The rough grey walls of the church and the moss-covered gravestones in the oldest part of the graveyard were silent witnesses to how old the little building was. She felt the eyes of people on her back as she made her way down the aisle to an empty pew. The sermon was short and pertinent. The singing was hearty, if not always in key, and the choice of hymns good and traditional. She was pleased when people greeted her as she made her way out through the lychgate.

'Amy! Amy!' A voice halted her. It was Ben's mother. She hastened to catch up with Amy, and a tall grey-haired man with dark friendly eyes followed her at a more leisurely pace. 'Hello! Lovely to see you! This is my husband!' She turned to him, filling in information of who Amy was as she said so. 'I told you about Amy the other day. She's Sally's great-niece and she's taken over *Rose Cottage*! Ben's friend!'

He held out his hand and his voice was deep and friendly. 'How do you do! I remember your aunt very well. She was a great supporter and helper of the church in her active lifetime. Like me she also was a member of the parish council. We miss her.' He smiled quietly at Amy.

Ben's mother turned to Amy. 'You must come for a meal! Next time Ben says he's coming, I'll get in touch.'

Amy felt uncomfortable. 'I'd rather not intrude . . . although it's a very kind thought of course.'

Brushing Amy's protest aside she

said, 'Nonsense! Ben pops in often since he started work on your cottage. I know he likes you, otherwise he wouldn't mention your name so often.'

Amy's voice was rough in her throat. 'Really?' She was lost for words and was glad when another couple caught Marjorie's attention. Ben's mother smiled and touched Amy's arm in parting, before turning towards them. 'I'll be in touch, Amy.'

The comfortable living-room with its dark furniture and floral chintz curtains was bathed in a warm golden haze from several table lamps. There was a pleasing smell of lavender-polish in the air, and floral arrangements of large pale-cream and yellow dahlias stood on the occasional table, and a mahogany sideboard.

They'd just finished a tasty meal and were now sitting in comfortable chairs talking about generalities. Among other things, they'd talked about Aunt Sally, about the village, and about the work on *Rose Cottage*. Amy took a sip of white wine. She concentrated on what Ben's father was saying and forced herself not to look in Ben's direction too often, although the temptation was almost to much.

Ben eyed her across the coffee table his hands caressing his wine glass. He looked very relaxed.

Eventually Amy glanced at her watch and stood up determinedly. 'Thanks for a lovely meal!'

Ben's mother nodded understandingly. 'You're welcome, my dear. Hope to see you again soon. Did you come by car?'

'No, but it'll only take me a couple of minutes to get home.'

His mother looked across. 'Ben?' She didn't need to say any more, he was already on his feet.

Amy felt flustered. 'Please, it's not necessary!'

Ben eyed her with an amused expression. 'I could do with some fresh air.'

Amy gave in gracefully; it was silly to

make a fuss. He followed her out to the hall and helped her into her jacket before she shook hands with his parents.

They followed the empty road that meandered through the centre of the small village. It was a mild evening, and the stars twinkled brightly in the black velvet sky. They threw their faint reflections on to the face of the pond, and the breeze brushed them into vague clusters of silver, as it wandered back and forth over the inky surface. The branches of the dark trees bordering the village green moved and rustled in the evening air.

The air was cold and invigorating after the warmth of the living-room, and Amy breathed deeply, before she broke the silence. 'You don't have to see me all the way home, Ben. I'll be all right.' She was very conscious of his tall figure ambling along comfortably at her side.

His face was hidden in the shadows. There was amusement in his voice. 'I wish you'd stop suggesting I'm being kind and considerate all the time. No-one forces me to do anything I don't want to do! It is quite likely that my mother has embarked yet again on her never-ending crusade to find me a wife, and she's now pin-pointed you as a likely candidate, but don't worry, I don't take any notice.' In the darkness, the outline of his shoulders lifted and fell as he shrugged. 'I could have taken my car, dropped you off and drove on if I wanted to get rid of you quickly.'

She was glad he couldn't see the colour rise in her cheeks. 'I like your parents.'

'Do you? Good.'

They continued to amble along. 'What was it like growing up in this village?'

'On the whole it was great. It was a bit inhibiting when we were teenagers because of its isolation. The bus service was abysmal, and so we were always dependent on parents picking us up from town all the time. That was annoying until some of us got a driving licence, but we managed.'

Amy thrust her hands deeper into the pockets of her jacket.

His voice grew more serious. 'Any more strange movements round the cottage?'

'Not that I've noticed! Don't make me nervous by bringing that up again!'

'I'm just being curious, that's all! Oh! — I've heard from the door and window company. They need a little more time to sort out the safety-touch button panel for the door. Not many people have ever asked for one, which means it'll take a week or two longer.'

Amy's heart sank. 'Oh! Pity!' She manage to make her voice sound matter of fact. 'But a couple of weeks one way or the other won't make much difference now.' Amy listened to their feet crunching on the road's gravelled surface.

He continued. 'Is everything OK otherwise?'

Amy hurried to reassure him. 'Yes,

fine!' They'd reached the cottage gate. Amy took a torch out of her pocket. 'Will the extra work on the drainage ditches push up the costs much? I just hope I've enough money to cover everything. I hoped I'd have enough to buy some old furniture when everything was finished, but I think I can forget that idea.'

'I've a friend with an antique business. Remind me to give you his card.'

'I can't afford antiques, Ben. I'm talking about inexpensive items.'

'Nice old furniture doesn't need to be out of reach of us all. Sometimes you just need patience. Josh deals in all kinds of stuff. If he knows what you want, he'll keep his eyes open. He takes his percentage of course, but he's fair. What are you looking for?'

Her voice was enthusiastic. 'A small side-table for the hall and I'd love an antique writing desk for the living-room, instead of Aunt Sally's long dark sideboard. Something smaller would look a lot better.'

His white teeth flashed in the darkness. 'I agree; it'd make the room look bigger.'

'Aunt Sally had a couple of old kitchen chairs and other bits and pieces up in the attic; the men brought them down and put them in the outhouse when they did the roof. There are two identical chairs, but they're both broken and damaged. I was wondering if I could make one decent one out of them for the hall. I'll have to find out about how to sand down and how to join things together, but . . . '

'Show me!'

'Now?'

'There's light in the outhouse, isn't there?'

8

Amy wished she hadn't mentioned it; in case it was just a foolish idea. She led the way, and the torch cut the darkness as they picked their way through the devastated garden. She buttoned the collar of her coat tighter and was grateful for her warm polo neck sweater. Once they were in the outhouse, she reached for the switch and they both blinked in the ensuing light. She walked to one of the corners where some bits and pieces of dilapidated chairs stood neglected and waiting for attention. Ben followed her, and viewed them sceptically.

'Hmm! Old Windsor chairs by the look.' He bent down and squatted to take a closer look. 'Probably need to take them completely apart, but at least they don't seem to have any woodworm.'

Amy nodded enthusiastically; her eyes

were bright with imagination of how a renovated chair would look next to a small table in the hallway.

'What are they?' He pointed to some picture frames propped up against the wall.

Amy looked. 'Oh, some dreary pictures of cows in the countryside; they were up in the attic with the chairs. They're so dismal and dark you can't see properly what's on them. I'll throw them in the skip next time.'

Ben shoved the pieces of chairs aside and pulled out the two pictures. He disturbed dust as he did so, and a faint musty smell filled the air as he stood up with the pictures. Holding them at arm's length, and peering closely, he said. 'Oil, and in a pretty good condition considering. I see what you mean about dreary-looking. Who knows, they might be worth something! I'd get them checked before you throw them away.'

'Are you kidding? You can't even make out what's supposed to be on them!'

'It looks like a pastoral scene to me.

That was a very popular theme in Victorian times, and would fit to the age of the cottage. Tell you what . . . I'll ask Josh to call. He's not an art expert, but he knows the right people. He can take a look at your chairs at the same time, and he might be able to find someone to put one together for a decent price.' He lifted the pictures. 'You'd better take them into the house until you know. The damp out here won't do them any good.'

Amy looked at him doubtfully, but she decided there was no point in arguing and picked her way ahead of him carefully down the remaining pathway. Over her shoulder, she said. 'You'll warn him that I'm not here during the day?'

He nodded and stepped inside the house briefly to stack the pictures against the wall. 'Lock up! Goodnight Amy. I'll let you know about the doors and windows as soon as I can pin the company to a definite date.'

His eyes were unfathomable, and

suddenly she wished she could think of a feasible reason to keep him with her for a few moments longer. There was a silence. She just nodded and said, 'Thanks for seeing me home! Goodnight, Ben! Want to borrow a torch?'

'No, there's enough light to see my way to the gate.' He turned away. Amy waited until he lifted his hand in farewell at the road. She locked the door, and tried the handle. She felt an urge to look out of the window to see where he was, but she resisted.

Marie invited herself to lunch the following week again despite Amy's warning over the phone that she didn't have anything to eat. 'I haven't been shopping this weekend yet. Have you saved your appetite in the hope of eating me out of house and home?'

'No I haven't! I'm not a scrounger! You must have something in the fridge?'

'Not much. Some cheese, and I've still got some apples. That's about it.'

Amy sighed silently. 'How will you get here?'

'The bus! It doesn't take long actually; I checked the times yesterday. I hoped that Ben would give me a lift, but he's visiting a friend of his.'

'Is he?' Amy was surprised, Marie had informed herself about the bus, and she didn't dare ask Marie questions about Ben, or the green-eyed monster might raise his jealous head. It was easier to try to ignore the possibility that Marie and Ben might be more than friends.

The two girls sat on opposite sides of the kitchen munching contentedly on some apples and catching up on each other's life. Amy avoided mentioning Ben, apart from his mother's invitation to a meal. The information didn't seem to bother Marie.

Amy's concentration heightened whenever Marie mentioned him, because she seemed to know a lot about Ben. Amy didn't ask too many questions and couldn't figure out how regularly they saw one another, but from what she gathered, Marie saw him quite often around town.

Amy knew that might not mean much. Once Marie got to know someone and liked them, she incorporated them into her life.

Marie made a general sweep with her arm. 'You're making progress. This place is beginning to look habitable again. Must be costing you a bomb. I'm glad I live in someone else's place; I'd go bonkers if I had to worry about repairs, improvements or replacements all the time. I'd rather invest my money in a Gucci bag. Paying rent is a drag, but . . . '

Amy bit her lip. 'I just hope that the work finishes before the money does. I don't know what I'll do if I can't pay.'

'I thought you had a loan from the bank?'

'I have, but the money just seems to disappear at an amazing rate. Ben says it's still all within the budget, but the biggest bills are still to come. When I sit down to pay the bills I sometimes break out in a sweat.'

Marie's black hair swung back and

forth as she shook her head. 'If Ben says things are OK, they're OK. Don't worry, and if they do go wrong, blame him. Take him to court for lulling you into acting falsely because he gave you the wrong information!'

Amy smiled. 'You're an inhuman hussy! As if I could! I thought you liked Ben?'

'You're too soft, Amy! You should learn to be more egotistical. Liking someone has nothing to do with protecting your own interests.'

Amy changed the subject. 'Rehearsal this afternoon?'

'Yes, but not for this play. For the next one, and I've got a bigger part — I'm the main supporting actress this time. I could take on the leading lady but that brainless man doesn't recognise talent when he sees it.'

'I presume you're talking about Henry again?'

'Yes, who else? Henry the 'know-it-all better man'.'

Amy sighed. It was hard to sympathise all the time. 'Marie, why aren't you just grateful that you have a bigger part? You were complaining that you didn't have a chance to show what you can do, and even though Henry is moving you up the ladder, all you can do is grizzle.'

Marie looked down, but didn't answer.

'I met Susan the other day and when his name came up she said how much better the motivation in the group was since he took it over, and how everyone admired his skills. You promised to give him a fair chance, remember?'

'Hmm!' Marie threw her stump into the waste bin with more force than necessary and didn't reply.

'I can't remember you ever reacting like this before. The trouble is that you're so used to men falling and grovelling at your feet, you can't stand it if one of them treats you like a normal human being. You say you love acting, and I can see that you're good at it! Don't make it difficult for you, or for him! He could easily throw you out if

122

you push him too far, and where will you be then?'

Marie looked thoughtful and her voice was gentle for a change. 'I try to be reasonable, but then the fuse explodes and I tell him all kind of things he doesn't want to hear.' She paused and looked at her cousin wistfully. 'I want to act so much, Amy, this is what I've been looking for! I love acting.'

Amy almost felt sorry for her. It was the first time Amy had heard Marie more or less admitting she'd spent too many years doing things that she didn't like. 'Then pull yourself together and keep your temper under control. You don't have to love him, or he you; you only have to work together.'

'Are you mad! Who's talking about love? He's the last man on this earth that interests me.' She got up. 'Be a gem and give me a lift back to town. You said you had to go shopping this afternoon. Coming out this evening? The gang is going out to that pub near Hawksbridge.'

Amy shook her head. 'I don't like coming back to the cottage in the dark on my own. When everything is finished, and the lighting in the garden is working, I won't mind so much.'

'Lighting? In the garden?'

Amy said proudly. 'The electrician is fixing garden spotlights to highlight the garden and the path.'

Marie lifted her eyebrows. 'Golly! It sounds like 'sans et lumière' in miniature! Are you going to have a 'switching-on' ceremony, like they do for the Blackpool lights? Start charging entrance fees — you might get your money back in about two hundred years time! Now, what about tonight? You're turning into a proper hermit! Come out with us; you can spend the night with me!'

Amy shook her head and smiled wryly. 'Your sofa had a couple of loose springs; the last time I slept there I needed a week to straighten my back out.'

* * *

Mike had succeeded in adding another big customer to their service list. He decided it was a reason to celebrate and took Amy out for lunch. They went to a small place in the High Street, which only had a couple of tables, but produced mouth-watering meals.

The meal was an all-round success and Amy felt very glad that she and Mike got on so well. He was her boss, but he was a nice man and a real friend, too. Later than business hours allowed, they headed arm in arm back to work. She was laughing at something Mike said when she spotted Ben walking towards them. He saw them at the same time and his step faltered for a second until he drew alongside. He gave Amy a polite smile and looked Mike over with deliberation.

Her heart did a quick somersault. Her colour heightened, 'Hello, Ben! On your lunch break?' Was it her imagination or was there an edge to his voice?

'No, on my way back to the office.'

She nodded. 'Oh this is Mike! Mike

this is Ben. Ben is in charge of the cottage conversion.'

Mike tipped his head in acknowledgement. 'You're making a good job of it.'

'That's what I'm paid to do; but I'm glad you approve.' He looked at his watch. 'Sorry, I have to rush. I've a client arriving in a couple of minutes!'

He was clearly impatient to get away. She nodded understandingly and tucked her hand through Mike's arm again. 'Of course. See you!'

He murmured, 'Umm! Bye, Amy!' and nodded towards Mike before he hurried off without a backward glance. It took a lot of her willpower not to turn to watch him go.

Josh, the antique dealer, turned up just after she got home on Tuesday the following week. He had reddish hair, light blue eyes, was in his forties, and his weathered skin showed that he spent a lot of time outdoors. 'Hi! Ben asked me to call, to look at some paintings and furniture.'

Amy motioned him to come in. 'I'm glad you've come when it's still light. You'll be able to see things better; the furniture is outside, the pictures are in here. What did Ben tell you?'

'That you had some dirty, indefinable paintings, and some grotty bits of furniture that you wanted done up.'

Amy tilted her head and laughed softly. 'I'm surprised you came at all after that.'

'Ben never wastes time on flattering vocabulary. Where are they?'

She spoke eagerly. 'The paintings are standing against the wall over there. The 'grotty furniture' is in the outhouse. Come in! Help yourself. I was just going to make myself a sandwich. Like one?'

He shook his head. 'Go ahead. I'll take a look at these in the meantime.'

She joined him again in the hall munching on a thick cheese sandwich. 'Well?'

He was holding one of the paintings aloft examining the back. 'Hmm! I don't want to build your hopes up too much, but these could be worth something. They need cleaning badly, but you can see it's a country lane arched by trees. No signature, but I wouldn't be surprised to find it's by a Victorian landscape painter called Edward Williams. He came from a family of painters who were active from 1800 until roughly 1880.

'I saw a similar one at an auction once and there was a picture in the catalogue of 'before and after cleaning'. It looked like this. The condition of the second one is not so good, and I'm not an expert on paintings, but if you trust me, I'll get an expert to take a look at them.'

Amy looked startled. 'Trust you? Ben recommended you — of course I do! To be honest, I was on the brink of throwing them away.'

He laughed and his eyes twinkled. 'Don't count on anything yet. I'm going to London next week, and I'll show them to someone who specialises in this period of English landscape paintings. Even if I'm right, they're not likely to be worth a fortune, but they might bring a decent sum at an auction.'

Her eyes shone. 'How wonderful!'

'Where's this furniture of yours?'

He followed in her footsteps. In the outhouse he looked sceptically at the bits of broken chairs in his hands. 'Well, they probably used to be nice Windsor Chairs, and I suppose if you take the best from each of the two chairs, you could make one decent one. Some of the parts are unfortunately warped. Look here! Luckily they probably come from the same origin, and there doesn't seem to be any woodworm so it might be possible to make one from the pieces.'

He paused. 'If the paintings turn out to be valuable paying someone to do your chair will also be the least of your worries!'

9

Amy saw Ben's car draw into the narrow bay in front of the cottage from the kitchen window and hurried to the door. Her smile widened as she watched him come up the path with a bottle in his hand. As he drew closer he waved it in the air. 'Josh phoned to tell me. I thought it was a good reason to celebrate.'

She nodded energetically. 'I still can't believe it. Come in!' She closed the door behind him and preceded him into the living room.

He gazed at her and followed her lithe figure. When she turned to face him, the colour in her cheeks heightened. He thought how the soft jade pullover flattered the creaminess of her face and the colour of her eyes.

'Josh left them in London to be restored. Then I can put them up for auction if I like.'

His tanned face emphasised the whiteness of his smile. 'And? Will you?' He lifted the bottle questioningly, and she got some long-stemmed glasses from the sideboard.

'One of them isn't in tip-top condition, but the other is. Both of them would sell, according to the expert, but the one would bring a lot more than the other. I'm thinking about keeping the best one and selling the other.'

He removed the gold wrapper from the neck, held the bottle at the base, and twisted slowly, easing out the cork and then pouring two glasses of champagne. He lifted his to her. His eyes were deep and unfathomable. 'You'll need extra insurance if you do, but I'm pleased for you, honestly! Here's to you and your paintings!'

She lifted her glass in return. 'And here's to you. I'd have thrown them away with the rubbish if it hadn't been for you!'

There were touches of humour near his dark eyes and the corner of his mouth turned up. 'It was just a lucky hunch, that's all!'

'I'll be able to buy a writing desk for the living room now.'

He nodded understandingly. 'Good idea! Oh! Marie mentioned you're worried that we'll overstep the budget? We won't, I'm keeping an eye on the costs.'

Amy looked down at the floor briefly, gripped the slender glass a little tighter, and looked up again, managing to shrug nonchalantly as she did so. She liked Marie a lot and she was more than halfway to loving Ben — she couldn't bear to band them together. 'I only mentioned it because the money seems to dwindle at an alarming rate. I wondered if I'd still be solvent before everything is finished.' She put the glass on the table and sat down in an armchair, indicating he should do the same.

He did, but she was even more

acutely conscious of his tall, athletic frame as he filled the chair opposite. He took another sip, and leaned forward to deposit his glass. Amy concentrated on the bubbles in her glass.

'I'm glad. Some people seem to ignore that aspect once they have a loan of money in their account.' He paused. 'I'm sticking to our financial plan Amy, if there's any danger of overstepping the mark I'll warn you long before it gets to be a headache.'

She pushed back a wayward strand of hair and nodded at him without speaking. She leaned back watching him, contentedly sipping the liquid now and then.

He broke the ensuing silence. 'So are you going to celebrate?' He grinned. 'Marie thought that a party would be most appropriate.'

Amy wrinkled her nose and shook her head. 'Trust Marie! No, not yet. Perhaps later when the garden is tidy, and the house is really finished.'

'They'll be filling the ditches this

week, and starting on the bathroom at the end of the week. Have you chosen tiles etc.?'

She got up and fetched brochures from a drawer. She spread the pages on the table and flipped through them to find what she'd chosen. 'I decided to take these fittings. What do you think?'

He leaned forward to study the pictures. Their heads were inches apart, and Amy's heart quickened.

'Perfect! Simple, an ageless design, not too bombastic, good quality. Tiling?'

'In white; the plumber brought some sample tiles last week.'

He nodded and leaned back. 'You know what you want, that's great. Nothing blocks progress more than customers who dilly-dally. It's more dirt and dust I'm afraid, but it'll be the last big mess.'

She laughed softly. 'Where have I heard that before?'

He shook his head, and grinned. 'I know — it must be depressing!'

She shrugged her shoulders. 'I

haven't got very far with my decorating, but there's no point in painting as long as there's dust in the air.'

He looked at her sympathetically. 'Have you been able to do anything at all?'

'It gets dark quickly, so by the time I get home I can't do much. So far, I've only finished the middle bedroom. I'm going to move in there on the weekend. When the bathroom's finished, I'll be able to take one room at a time, go through the whole house.'

She looked at the clock and hesitated before she ploughed on. 'Would you like something to eat? Nothing special — either an omelette and salad, or steak and chips?' Awkwardly she cleared her throat. 'Only if you don't have anything else planned for this evening, of course.'

He looked at her intently. 'A steak sounds great.'

The sun had gone, draining the light from the sky and leaving the cottage in semi-darkness. Outside, as the sun sank lower, the chilly autumn winds fretted at the ivy on the outhouse and shook the branches of the trees angrily. Inside Amy switched on the lights. A cosy atmosphere from the down-lights and table lamps ripened as muted light spread across the room. Ben made them a crisp green salad when Amy was frying the steaks; it was clear that he was used to preparing food, his movements were sure and efficient.

Amy felt completely relaxed as they sank into the soft armchairs in the living room afterwards with fresh ground coffee. Her mouth curved into an unconscious smile as they talked about everything and nothing. She was pleased to find they had lots in common, even if they didn't agree on everything.

Ben appraised her and was lost in his own thoughts as the conversation flowed.

They were both surprised at how fast time went, and he stood up reluctantly when he decided it was time to leave.

She didn't try to stop him. Outside the wind was quite strong, and it whipped her hair across her face.

He turned to her on the threshold. His face was hidden in the shadows. 'Don't hang around, it's cold! Thanks for the meal. I enjoyed it.'

She swallowed a lump in her throat, and stared at him. 'So did I. Drive carefully!'

He nodded. 'Lock the door, Amy!' He reached forward to push a strand of hair from her face, and bent quickly to kiss her cheek.

She smiled at him gently and, when he turned away, she closed and quickly locked the door. Her hand brushed the spot where his lips had touched her skin. Each time she saw him the attraction grew stronger. She resisted the urge to watch him from the window, and went through the cottage to turn out the lights, one by one.

Dust hung in the air everywhere every day the following week as the workers attacked what would be her future toilet and bathroom. She didn't even try to do more than vacuum the surface every evening; cleaning was a pointless pastime until all the dust had settled.

Shadows were creeping across the fields and following in their stead was a wide band of silver mist. Amy had sorted out some more small items she didn't intend to keep, and carried an over-brimming cardboard box to the outhouse to give them to someone for the Xmas bazaar in the village. Bert and his men were getting ready to leave. Amy supported the carton on her raised hip and reached out to switch on the light. A blue flash flared, and a jarring sensation shot up her arm for a few seconds and she dropped the box with a screech. 'Ouch!!'

Bert came across quickly; she was still rubbing her wrist. 'What was that?'

'I switched on the light and it exploded!'

'Lord above! Hurt bad?'

Amy studied her hand. 'It stunned

me more than anything else.'

Bert took a torch out of the bib of his dungarees and aimed the beam of light at the old-fashioned light switch. One of the cables was hanging loose; the light-switch and the surrounding area were charred and brown. The loose cable was not burned or marked, just hanging. He rubbed his chin. 'Hmm! You're lucky you weren't carrying something wet; that would have been really dangerous.'

Amy laughed unsteadily. 'This place needs modernisation inside as well as out!'

'Yes, so it seems. The cottage is re-wired, but I don't suppose the electrician thought of the wiring out here. I'll tell Ben about it tomorrow and he'll get on to the electrician again.'

'I suspect the electrician was planning to do it at the same time as he was going to install the lighting in the garden.'

Bert was still rubbing his chin thoughtfully. 'You're probably right, but it goes to show you can't take anything for granted — we've all been in and out of this place a hundred times, switching the light on and off, and nothing happened!'

Mike gave her permission to go early on Friday. He knew that she was longing to get home to clear up the pile of accumulated dust and dirt. He was following the progress of the cottage with interest and was impressed by how Amy was coping. Amy's heart skipped a beat when she saw Ben's car parked in the lane. He was talking to the plumber and gave her a smile when he saw her coming.

'Hi! You're home early!'

'Umm! I asked for an extra couple of hours off so that I can get to grips with some of the dust before nightfall. The workmen said they'll not be making any more dust, so I thought that I'd start giving the rooms a thorough clean-out again.'

He gave a throaty laugh and his eyes twinkled. 'Oh dear! I wish I had your optimism. It will be days before the dust really settles. You must enjoy housework!'

She looked a little crest-fallen, but answered quite brightly. 'Not much, but the work won't go away of its own accord; and I haven't got a fairy godmother to wave her wand. My mother offered to come and help, but it seems unfair to drag her all this way, just to work. I'd rather see her when everything is tidy and habitable.'

He looked down briefly and then studied her face. 'Bert told me you got a shock, from the light-switch in the outhouse?'

Amy wrinkled her nose. 'Oh, yes! The other day — almost forgot that! It's a good thing the wiring is being replaced.'

Ben held her glance steadily. 'Yes. Anything unusual otherwise?'

'Unusual? What do you mean unusual?'

'What I said; anything out of the ordinary. You're cut off from the village here.'

Amy thought briefly and hesitated

before she said, 'No, nothing special. I thought I heard something or someone moving around outside a couple of nights ago, but it could have been the wind or just my vivid imagination.'

His jaw tightened. 'Did you take a look?'

Amy laughed weakly. 'You're kidding? I didn't even have enough courage to look out of the bedroom window, never mind actually go outside.'

He nodded. 'Good. Don't be tempted, no matter what! It's probably just a fluke of imagination and the references to the ghost at the back of your mind, but there is no point in trying to be heroic. Keep the door locked!'

Amy's eyes widened. 'You're making me more nervous than ever!'

He hooked his hands in his pockets and tried to sound nonchalant. 'That's not my intention, but it's sensible to take precautions, for perfectly obvious reasons!' Ben motioned towards the plumber. 'I've been going over things with Bob. Things are going according to plan, and with a little luck he'll be out of here in ten days or so.'

It was getting better. Every day when she came home, progress was noticeable; the building chaos was receding and she had a home again. The dust had settled, and although the men were still finishing the bathroom, her cleaning efforts made inroads at last. And . . . they had a definite delivery date for the door and the windows at last!

Amy mused that when the house was finished, it wasn't very likely that she'd see much of Ben any more. She'd thoroughly cleaned the rooms that were finished, and now she only needed to clean the remaining rooms when the workmen finally finished their job. That weekend she noticed herself how much cleaner and shiny things were.

She got up early on Saturday and had already managed to get through a lot of work by lunchtime. The shopping for the week ahead was stored away, and washing was blowing outside in the cold wind.

She hurried through a quick lunch of sandwiches so that she could go to the DIY centre to buy some paint. It felt wonderful to be thinking about something creative for a change and not just about dirt and mess.

10

A couple of hours later she drove her car with ease into the narrow space next to the hedge. She got out of her car, and opened the boot. Lifting as much as she could comfortably carry in one go, she transported it indoors and piled it on the floor in the hall. She straightened up and returned for the rest. Amy had to lean further into the back of the boot to reach for some tins of paint, so when a rough voice drifted over her shoulder it frightened her out of her wits.

'Anything to spare lady! For a poor man who's down on his luck?'

Amy stepped back at the double, hitting her head on the lid of the boot as she did so. It wasn't a hard whack, although her heart began to race and the colour left her face as she looked and saw a dishevelled man in dirty clothes and a greasy trilby hat watching her closely. He eyed her and then the house, and its open door.

'Uh! I . . . I . . . Pardon?' She tried to sound at ease, and wished for the umpteenth time since she moved in to the cottage that it wasn't so cut-off from the village.

His eyes were small pieces of black coal, piercing and crafty. 'A bit of money for some food perhaps? Or even a roof over my head for the night — that outhouse would suit me fine.'

A cold shiver ran down her back and she wondered how she could get rid of him. She didn't want him anywhere near the house — especially not overnight. Amy had dumped her shoulder bag on the floor in the hall with the first load of goods. She quickly decided the only way she could get rid of him was to give him a couple of pounds, and hope he'd then be satisfied, and go away. 'Wait here!'

He looked around furtively and began to feel more confident. There was no sign of anyone else about the place or close at hand and he could tell she was hoping to fob him off; he had enough time to scare her a bit more. 'How about a hot cup of tea and a sandwich, Miss?'

Slowly Amy felt how panic was building inside and how her stomach knotted tighter. She felt increasingly afraid of him, of his leering expression, and she thought that it might not be easy to get rid of him. His rough appearance and belligerent facial expression made her nervous. If someone like him had confronted her in town, she'd have given him some small change, or tried to avoid him. Here she felt vulnerable, and under threat from the way he was staring at her, and the house.

Her hand went to her throat; how could she get rid of him without him noticing she was scared? As the thoughts tumbled through her brain, she spotted Ben's car sailing around the bend and all her anxieties melted away. Amy had never felt more relieved in her life than when his car came to a gentle stop behind hers. She was so thankful to see him that she didn't notice that the tramp had taken to his heels, hurrying through the garden and the gap in the hedge behind the cottage and heading across the field into the distance.

Ben climbed out, slammed the door and came towards her. The developing smile died when he noticed the concerned apprehensive expression. He looked at the disappearing man now fading quickly into the distance. 'Who was that? Is something wrong, Amy?'

Amy looked around for the tramp, and was surprised to find herself alone with Ben, and no sign of the unwelcome visitor. Her stomach was clenched up tight, and she hoped she could explain what had happened without sounding silly. 'A tramp. He didn't threaten me or anything, not with words . . . but somehow I . . . '

He waited silently, eyeing her carefully and listening to the anxiety in her voice.

' . . . I felt almost frightened! He was

only a tramp; it was silly of me.' She gave a weak laugh and coloured — it brought some colour back to her face again. 'He must have disappeared as soon as he noticed your car. I didn't even see him go.' She picked up the paint tins where they'd fallen back into the boot, to cover her embarrassment.

Her words didn't fool Ben. His eyes swept the garden and his voice was serious. 'Look, Amy, the doors and windows will probably be here next week, but I think you need company for a while. Living here on your own is not a good idea unless you feel safe.' He took a good look around. 'Whoever he was, he's not here any more. He probably was just a harmless tramp, and perhaps you interpreted his actions in the wrong way.'

He put up his hand to stop her protest. 'He saw you were nervous and alone and tried to put some pressure to take advantage of you.' He paused. 'I think it's better if someone stays here for a while until the doors and windows are properly fitted.' Reaching over to relieve her of one of the paint tins, he said firmly, 'Come on, I'll make you a cup of tea.'

Amy already felt a lot better, and wished she hadn't been so daft. His presence gave her the support and comfort she needed. In the kitchen, he put on the kettle and she got the cups.

Ben talked as he worked. 'I'll pick up what I need for a couple of days after some tea.'

'Wha . . . what? What did you say?'

'I'll get enough stuff for a couple of days.' He sounded very casual.

She was momentarily speechless with surprise. 'You can't move in with me!'

He took charge of the situation with quiet assurance. 'Why ever not? Or do you want to ask someone else?'

'Ben! I'm sure you've better things to do than to play guardian angel just because a tramp scared me! He's not likely to come back again now. I'll be all right.'

'Let me decide that. I'll feel better if

I'm around to keep an eye on you; too many things have happened here recently . . . I'll stay until things are really secure.'

The colour flooded her cheeks as she thought about the nearby village and possible gossiping. 'What will your mother think?'

'Does it matter what she thinks? Are you planning to phone her and tell her I'm here?' He stood solidly waiting for her answer. 'It's all perfectly innocent. Even if it wasn't, it's none of her business. Want me to stay, or not?'

She didn't need to think twice, her answer was instant. 'I'd like you to, if it's not too much trouble!'

When Ben drove off to pick up his things, Amy was so agitated that she phoned Marie. She didn't want Marie to find out that Ben was staying at the cottage by chance. Amy didn't want her to think she was elbowing-in or trying to out-manoeuvre her in any way if Marie and Ben were close.

She explained what had happened.

Marie gave Amy some colourful descriptions of what she would have told the tramp, but Ben's intended arrival didn't seem to bother Marie; in fact she sounded buoyant and seemed to be in a very good mood.

'Keep your eye on Ben though!' Marie chuckled. 'It may all be part of a diabolical plan of his so that he can buy the cottage up cheap when it comes on to the market. No-one knows better than he does how much it's worth now!'

'Oh, Marie!' Amy wondered if her acting was affecting her cousin's brain. 'Don't talk rubbish! Ben wouldn't be so underhand; why should he?'

'Why is anyone underhanded? Mostly to make money, of course!'

'Ben's not like that!' She couldn't keep the defiant tone out of her voice.

'Darling all men are like that; and a lot of women are too. We are carnivorous beasts when the time, the reason and the opportunity is ripe.'

Amy's first thought was where she could put Ben to sleep. She had an inflatable mattress and he'd have to manage with that. She hadn't got round to replacing the old mattresses she'd thrown away. She was still waiting to decide if she'd keep any of the old fashioned bed-frames and would then need replacement mattresses.

When Ben returned, she was annoyed that she felt smidgens of embarrassment about the situation. Standing in the hallway, he had a bulging holdall in one hand and his laptop and briefcase in the other. The warmth of his smile echoed in his voice. 'I take it that I'm in the spare room down the end?'

'That's mine. You can have the main bedroom. I've made up a bed. It's a bit spartan but I hope you'll be comfortable.'

An arched brow showed his humorous acceptance. 'I'm sure I will.'

'Make yourself at home, Ben!' She twisted her hands nervously together. 'And . . . and thank you for coming. Your presence will give me peace of mind until they've fitted the door and windows.'

He nodded without commenting. 'I'll

take my bag upstairs. I've brought some work with me; I have to finish it over the weekend.'

'Then carry on. Use the dining-room or kitchen table, just as you please.'

They shared a smile and he turned away to climb the stairs.

It was easy having him around and she could secretly watch him with smug delight. He was soon absorbed in his work, and Amy decided to get the preparation for painting her walk-in-wardrobe out of the way.

Later, he heard the sounds of saucepans and cooking in the kitchen. His voice echoed down the corridor. 'Need any help?'

She felt light-hearted. 'No, carry on! I'd planned to make a chicken casserole for this evening, OK with you?' Amy had added some extra sage and thyme and juicy tomatoes; the smell of the fresh herbs was good. She put the kettle on to make some instant stock.

'Sounds great! I volunteer to do the washing up!'

Daylight was fading by the time she opened a bottle of white wine and set the table. Their meal was relaxed and companionable. She'd always felt good in his company, even though she always felt emotionally nervous. His presence across the table was something that gave her immeasurable pleasure although she was careful not to let her thoughts wander too far.

They shared the task of washing up, and then they carried the rest of the wine with them as they both went into the living room — him to his work, and Amy to a book she was reading. Easy silence reigned, although Amy couldn't help stealing a glance at him now and then, as she sipped on her glass and read the same page for the umpteenth time without understanding a word.

After a leisurely breakfast next morning, he took a quick look at the walk-in wardrobe, and then went back to his own tasks. Amy painted while listening to music coming from a portable radio, and she felt quite elated.

The mere knowledge that he was downstairs was something that gave her bottomless peace and satisfaction. By lunchtime, the painting was finished.

Ben was wearing a washed out T-shirt and a comfortable pair of trainers. He leaned backwards in his chair and crossed his arms behind his head. He smiled and her heart fluttered. 'You're spoiling me, Amy. Much more of this and I'll move in for good!'

She blushed. 'It's the least I can do. It's only a couple of sandwiches and some coffee.'

Amy went out to rake rubbish in the garden. It was a bright day full of early winter sunshine. There was a weak contemptuous wind that troubled her anorak and scarf as she tried to gather heaps of leaves together. The wind blew them helter-skelter again in no time, and she soon realised she was fighting windmills. Her cheeks were soon glowing, and they reddened even more when she spotted Ben watching her from the window. Her breath was coming in white puffs as she raked and tidied. She wasn't expecting visitors.

'Hello, Amy!' The voice shook her daydreams. Amy looked up; it was Ben's mother.

'Elsie told me Ben's car was here, and as I wanted to see him anyway to tell him my cousin, Arthur, has died, I thought you wouldn't mind . . . ?'

'No . . . no, of course not. I . . . come inside!' Amy couldn't decide whether to explain his presence or not. She stood the rake against the wall and led the way. Just when they entered the hall, he was coming downstairs. In his casual clothes and socks on his feet, the picture was very 'at home'.

Marjorie looked at him, and then pointedly at Amy but she didn't say anything, and moved towards the living room. Amy turned a deeper shade of pink, and decided to leave it to Ben to explain. She made a hasty exit.

It was a completely different feeling to come home knowing that Ben was around. She felt secure, happy and confident. She even began to hope there'd be a longer delay with the windows and doors. To Amy's surprise, Marie turned up one evening with Henry. They brought some smoked salmon and wine.

Marie was in top form and Henry seemed happy with life too, so they'd clearly buried their differences. The two girls went into the kitchen to arrange the salmon on plates and cut wedges of fresh crisp baguette.

Amy hissed quietly. 'I thought you couldn't stand Henry?'

'He has a car, and when I said I wanted to see you and needed a lift, he more or less offered to drive me here and invited himself in into the bargain.' Marie licked her fingers, shook them under the water tap, and then dried them on a teacloth.

Amy looked towards the living room, and listened briefly to the murmur of voices. 'But what about 'macho' 'brain-less' and all the other adjectives you used?'

Marie looked a little sheepish, and arranged the bread in the basket. 'Oh, he does improve on closer acquaintance.' Noticing Amy's grin, she added hastily, 'But I'm still deciding if he deserves any special attention. Don't jump to conclusions!'

Amy liked Henry, so she enjoyed the evening very much. She wondered how Ben felt about Marie turning up with another man, but if he cared, he didn't show it. It was a nice evening with a lot of laughter and enjoyable chatter.

Marie was as lively as ever. Amy was almost sure she noticed how Marie's eyes lingered too often on Henry's face. Amy bubbled with laughter inside. She couldn't help noting how Henry handled Marie. It was almost more appropriate to use the word 'manipulated' because Amy was sure that Marie wasn't aware of the fact that for once she wasn't in the driving seat!

11

The house was finished; the small casement windows were snugly fitted, and the door with its safety panel was functioning perfectly. There was no reason for Ben to remain; for him to act as her protector any more. Amy pretended she was happy about everything.

The day Ben moved out they shared an unusually quiet breakfast. Until today they'd always shared bits of conversation across the pages of the newspapers. Now Ben's head was stuck in his paper. He ate his usual two slices of crisp toast, covered in thick marmalade and absentmindedly finished his mug of coffee quickly.

Amy was busy with her bowl of cereal, and wondered why it tasted like cardboard. She avoided glancing in his direction, and sipped her tea while flipping through the pages of her favourite woman's magazine without registering a word. The rustle of the newspaper as he folded it neatly together caught her attention; he stood up.

'Well, I'll be off.' His voice gave nothing away. Amy couldn't decide whether he was happy or reluctant to leave. 'You're pretty safe now, and as long as you take the usual kind of precautions, I'm sure you'll be all right.' He gave her a crooked grin. 'Apart from the ghost of course!'

Amy nodded like an automat and concentrated her attention long enough to answer. 'I'm planning to give her a cup of tea and some biscuits next time she shows up.'

'Then buy chocolate ones, no-one can resist those.' He looked more serious. 'You have my number, if there's any more trouble.' He stuck the newspaper under his arm.

With a lump in her throat, but with no noticeable change to her voice she looked up at him and said. 'Thanks, Ben. Thanks for everything, not just for staying with me for the last week or so. The cottage is just as I thought it would be, and I know that's mainly because you did your job so well.'

The corners of his mouth turned up as he studied the jade coloured eyes. He gave her a crooked smile. 'I hope you'll still think as kindly when I send you my final bill!' To her surprise he brushed her cheek lightly with a finger, and it took all Amy's self-control not to shrink away at his touch. 'Take care of yourself; you're one of my favourite clients, Amy Austin.'

Amy couldn't think of the right words on the spur of the moment and was afraid to answer in case she said something silly, and he might notice how special he was in her eyes. If she used the wrong words he might even be embarrassed, so she said nothing. He turned and picked up his holdall waiting by the kitchen door. He lifted a roll of plans in farewell before he bent slightly and went through the front door.

Amy watched him walk down the pathway to his parked car. The wind was fresh; it was tugging at his jacket, and ruffling his hair. Amy already knew how she'd miss him even though he wasn't yet out of sight. A few days in his company had only confirmed her belief that Ben was the man she wanted to spend the rest of her life with. He liked her, she sensed that, but liking wasn't enough for Amy. She needed his love to make her dreams come true.

Amy waited until the sound of his car faded into the distance. Her heart slumped and she cleared the table. She held his mug too long before she finally thrust it into the warm suds in the sink and washed it vigorously. She told herself not to be so silly, as she dried their dishes and put them away in the cupboard. She closed the door with an audible bang.

The next couple of days were a muddle of adjusting to the fact that she wouldn't see Ben much (if ever) again. The realisation that he was gone from her life made her so miserable that it was almost a physical pain. She had never seen him in town before the renovation of the cottage, and the likelihood of seeing him after was just as unlikely. She certainly didn't intend to go out of her way to look for him like a love-struck teen.

The first day it seemed so quiet in the cottage when she got home from work that loneliness engulfed her, and she gulped hard to stop the tears flowing. Parallel with Ben's departure all the other building activities had also come to an abrupt end. No more workmen, no more interruptions. The cottage, including the new bathroom and WC looked beautiful and she was proud of it.

Once she'd finally finished the remaining decorating and the garden was laid, her home would leave nothing to be desired. She was already extraordinarily proud of it.

She kept a smile on her face but even Mike noticed the difference. It was nothing he could put his finger on, but he could tell something was bothering her. He'd known her too long not to ask tentatively if she was all right, but she assured him she was fine. Mike decided she'd tell him when she was ready; he respected her privacy. Her father's death had knocked her sideways a couple of years ago, and it took a while until she could talk about that.

The days passed, and the ache remained, but gradually Amy came to terms with the situation. It was a huge painful knot inside. On one hand she ached to see him and wished he would phone just so she could hear his voice, but on the other she hoped he wouldn't, because it would only cause her pain again.

Keeping herself busy was the best way of not dwelling too much on Ben. Life went on, and she needed something to occupy her time. She'd start with the rest of the decorating; that might distract her thoughts a bit. She hadn't heard from Marie for a while — a visit to Marie would also help pull her out of the doldrums for a couple of hours.

Amy was curious to know how Marie and Henry were getting along. Even if Amy felt miserable about her own life at the moment, she still hoped that Marie had found a worthwhile relationship. Henry was just the right kind of man for her cousin.

Early on Saturday morning she drove to the DIY centre to stock up on paint and filler. It was already busy when she got there. She knew that the weekend wasn't the best time to do her shopping, but it was getting dark when she got home after work in the week, and she wanted daylight to decide on colours.

She looked around for a suitable space to park and was lucky to find one not far from the entrance. She locked the car and walked briskly towards the shop entrance. Suddenly a car drove out of a row of parked vehicles. As if she was watching a slow-motion movie, Amy saw it was coming directly at her. Her brain seemed to be paralysed, and although she knew she had to get out of the way, she stared at it for fractions of a second like a snake watching a mongoose.

She thrust out her arm instinctively to hold the car at bay, but it didn't brake and didn't seem to care that a person was in the way. Amy reacted at last, jerking to the side, her hip curving away from the oncoming car in an instinctive movement. The car's mudguard caught her and she still couldn't believe it was happening.

The impact knocked her sideways and she finally landed with a thud. Her shoulder jarred and she slid roughly across the uneven surface. A collection of empty trolleys finally stopped her progress. Breathless, she struggled to her knees, and felt her chest hurting as she began to take short gasps of air. Still adjusting to what had happened, and still not believing it actually had taken place, she tried to stand.

Some people gathered and the restraining hand of a woman on her shoulders kept her where she was. In the background she heard the accelerating drone of an engine as the car drove off.

The woman's voice was shocked. 'Did you ever! He's making off! He's not stopping!'

A man's voice said loudly. 'What a cheeky beggar! You're not safe anywhere these days. He was driving much too fast; this is a parking lot, not a speedway track!'

Another woman made a quick suggestion. 'Someone ought to get his number! Hey, our Jack — run lad! Cut through the rows to the exit. He has to drive to the end of the building before he can turn. Get a look at his number, and try to remember as much of it as you can. Be careful, but try to catch him.'

From the sound of pounding feet,

Amy gathered that Jack was doing as he was told.

The same voice bent down and went on. 'How are you, love? No, stay where you are, don't get up. Anyone got a phone?'

Someone said. 'Yes.'

'Phone the police and tell them we need an ambulance too.'

Amy opened her mouth to protest. She didn't want a fuss; she felt rather stupid.

'Take it easy, love! Let a doctor check you over. You might feel OK, but it's only sensible to be sure! That was a nasty fall you took.'

At the hospital she'd been examined in the accident unit, and they'd taken some X-rays. The doctor on duty announced she'd been lucky and only had some minor injuries, and suspected concussion. Amy was feeling a lot better already, and wanted to go home, but she gave in after he told her it was a sensible precaution to stay overnight.

They gave her a bed in a general

ward, and something to send her to sleep. Before she felt too drowsy she'd been able to make one telephone call. She left a message on Marie's answering machine, telling her where she was and why, and she also warned Marie not to worry her mother. She was OK!

When she woke next morning, it took Amy a couple of seconds to remember why she was lying in a hospital bed in a hospital gown. There was a clatter of a trolley outside in the corridor and movements in neighbouring beds. The scent of dahlias wafted from further down the ward If she shifted around, her stiff bruised body protested. She was very thirsty and longed for something to drink. Amy smoothed down her hair and struggled to sit up.

A ward sister on her rounds with a surgical tray in her hands, looked across at Amy in passing. She stopped by Amy's bed. 'Morning! How are you feeling?'

Amy replied honestly. 'A bit stiff, but perfectly OK otherwise thanks!'

'Headache? Dizziness? Feel sick?'

'No.'

'That's good. Apart from bruises, lots of scratches, and a cracked rib you were lucky.'

Amy smiled up at the young woman. 'I feel a bit of a fraud this morning.'

'You should be grateful that you got off so lightly — it could have been a lot worse.'

'Can I get up? Get dressed, and go home?'

'Hang on a bit, until the doctor has done his rounds, and given you the all clear.' She noted Amy's resigned expression. 'I'll send in your visitor, to keep you company for a while.'

'Visitor?' Amy was puzzled; Marie must have broken all records and got up early.

'He's very impatient and if I keep him out much longer he'll wear a groove in the corridor floor from walking up and down all the time.' Amy had no time to ask any more questions. Her starched apron rustled as she arranged the curtains and moved away.

Amy looked expectantly towards the door, and surprise siphoned the remaining blood from her already pale face as Ben's figure rounded the door. His eyes ran the length of the half-empty ward and found her. Their eyes met and they exchanged a message that neither of them yet understood. A few long strides and he was by her side. Intense and honest astonishment covered her face.

'Ben! What are you doing here?' Her heart swelled with a feeling she'd tried to ignore. Any defences she'd managed to erect since she last saw him disintegrated completely.

Nervously he replied while studying her face closely. 'I had to see how you were.'

She swallowed with difficulty. 'Who told you I was here?'

'Marie.'

Amy stiffened. 'Marie shouldn't have bothered you.' Her eyes fixed on him towering above her.

He shook his head. 'She didn't bother me. She knew how much I'd want to know.'

Torn by the conflicting emotions whizzing around her brain, she tried to sound exasperated. 'I am not your responsibility. It was silly of Marie to get you involved.' She lowered her gaze in confusion. The white pallor of her skin made her look more vulnerable.

'I wish I was responsible for you.'

She looked up quickly not quite understanding. Her feelings whirled and skidded. He sat down on the edge of the bed and took her hand; his fingers sent pleasant jolts through her.

Her eyes were wide, she was taken aback, and Ben knew he'd gone too far to leave all the rest unspoken. 'I thank God that you weren't seriously injured; I was worried to death when I heard.'

A swift shadow of uncertainty swept through the brown eyes. 'Matter of fact I was already wondering how I could settle things with you, before this happened. Perhaps it's a wink from fate that I get the chance today!' There was a pause.

Amy stared at him tongue-tied wondering where his words were heading, but still managing to answer politely. 'Oh?'

He hesitated a moment again and ploughed on. 'Where do I begin? I suppose I could simply say I didn't realise how empty my life was till I met you.'

Amy drew an audible breath.

He was still nervous but his determination was growing. It was now or never. 'Everything I thought I was happy doing alone, made me feel discontented and empty, because all the time I only imagined how much more I'd enjoy it, if I was with you.'

A bubble of joy began to form inside, and with her mind spinning Amy listened to the words she'd dreamed he'd say.

'I love you, Amy.'

Euphoria and a new kind of warmth

spread through her. 'You love me?' She still couldn't believe it.

'Fate led me to Amy Austin and *Rose Cottage*. Once I fell in love with you there was no turning back.'

The happiness shone in her eyes. She nodded, 'I know!'

He listened with an uptight expression and a hint of uncertainty about him. She held his future in her hands and his jaw tensed visibly. 'Does that mean you love someone too?' He hesitated not wanting to hear an answer that would devastate his life. 'Who?'

She watched him for a second and a wide smile covered her face before she answered. 'Who do you think? You of course!'

A radiant smile transformed his expression and his eyes lit up. He bent and brushed a gentle kiss across her forehead. Her hair smelt of herbal shampoo. Then he gathered her into his arms gently, trying not to crush her, and kissed lips that were waiting and all too ready for his touch.

The feeling was delicious; he covered her lips with his hungrily again, and she kissed him back with all the loving and longing she'd hidden from him for so long. They looked into each other's eyes with expressions of equal amazement.

Ben pushed a stray strand of hair behind her ear and studied her closely. 'I wondered if I had a chance. Lord, I wish I'd tried to kiss you as often as I wanted to. I didn't know where I stood because my courage failed me all the time. I thought I needed a miracle, but didn't know where to look for one. You never gave me the slightest hint that you might welcome my attentions, other than in my professional capacity. I thought you might be in love with Mike!'

She laughed softly. 'And I thought you were in love with Marie, or with Julie!'

He was momentarily speechless. 'Julie? Julie comes in every couple of days to do the office work. She's happily married with two children. And

Marie? You can't be serious? I like her because it's like watching a bird of paradise in free flight, but I couldn't live with a firecracker like her, she'd drive me crazy! I want someone who glows steadily, someone who is kind and beautiful and reliable . . . I want you! I think I've felt that from that first evening you came to the office!'

He leaned to kiss her gently, holding her face between his hands. It was a featherlike kiss, and then his mouth covered hers hungrily when he felt Amy's eager response.

Very slowly, Amy came down to earth again and her mind began functioning again. Her face brightened noticeably, and an easy smile played at the corner of her mouth as she took a deep breath. 'It seems both of us picked up the wrong end of the stick. I thought you were attracted to Marie in the beginning, and later on someone called Julie answered your phone when I rang your flat one evening, and I thought she must be a special girlfriend.'

They were both slightly breathless.

Amy was coming out of the dark. 'Mike is my boss! He's a lovely chap and a good friend. He's about to marry his childhood sweetheart.'

He looked startled. 'You talked about your 'boss' and you mentioned 'Mike' but I didn't realise they were the same person!' The relief was audible in his voice.

She looked puzzled. 'Perhaps I never used the two words in the same sentence?' She took a deep breath and stared at him. 'Since you left me after that business with the tramp, I've missed you more than I can say. And I assure you I'm not in the habit of kissing men like I kissed you unless I love them.'

'And I want to spend the rest of my life with you, Amy, and I swear that I've never felt like that about anyone else before.'

Amy was astonished at the sense of fulfilment and happiness she felt. 'I can't believe this is happening!' Her jade eyes twinkled. 'I know it's wrong to think so, but I'm almost glad the accident happened, because it's brought us together, hasn't it?'

His lips tightened as his mind focussed on the accident again. He picked up her hands and fondled them. 'Amy! I have to tell you, although it isn't the right moment, I think you should know the truth. They've traced the car, and the man who drove it.' He paused.

'And?' She felt so happy that she was floating in space and didn't really care; she was still relishing the fact that Ben loved her. His hand held hers tightly.

'The man who was driving the car . . . it turns out that he is your uncle's batman.'

She stared at him in astonishment. 'Uncle Walter's batman? Gosh, what an amazing coincidence! Why did he bolt? He's an ex-soldier — it doesn't fit somehow.' She waited; her expression was full of interest and puzzlement.

He was silent.

Amy prompted. 'There's an explanation I suppose?'

Ben nodded silently. 'Apparently he did it intentionally!'

Amy drew in a quick breath.

'Apparently your Uncle Walter has been trying to buy a telescope that used to belong to the Duke of Wellington. He set his mind on it, and has been trying to persuade the present owners for a long time. Suddenly they agreed, but they wanted cash. Your uncle didn't have enough and so he tried to drag out the negotiations, but once these people had made up their minds they wanted it over and done with.

'They set him a deadline and threatened to put it up for auction. Soames, the batman, motivated by a misguided sense of loyalty to your uncle, thought that if he could frighten you out of the cottage it'd speed up Uncle Walter's prospects of getting his share of the cottage, and the bank would give him an advance loan. Soames broke down when the police confronted him.

'He also confessed he was responsible for the other 'accidents' you've had since you moved into the cottage; the loose carpet, the shock from the wiring in the outhouse, the suspicious activities outside the house . . . he was also the tramp that put the fear of God into you that day!'

A soft gasp escaped her soft lips and her eyes widened. 'He did all that just to frighten me out of the cottage?'

Ben nodded again. 'I know, it sounds like something from a second-rate film, doesn't it? Once the police traced the number of the car and cornered him with the truth, he admitted everything. Your uncle is terribly shocked; he didn't have a clue what was going on. Soames did it off his own back, and things got out of hand. Oh, before I forget . . . Marie isn't here because she thought as long as you weren't seriously injured, it was more important to see your uncle. She wormed all this information out of some young constable at the police station last night; otherwise we wouldn't have known the truth so quickly.'

Amy was too surprised to do more than nod.

'She said she was going to grab Henry and go round to see Uncle Walter. She phoned him when she discovered the truth, and apparently Uncle Walter sounded in a bad way. He was talking in confused circles. Marie said she knew you'd understand.'

Amy nodded. 'Of course. Poor Uncle Walter!'

Tongue in cheek Ben said, 'He'll need even more sympathy tomorrow. Marie's taking a bottle of whisky as well as comforting words; I expect he'll have an awful hangover!'

Amy guessed how shocked Uncle Walter must be. As far as Amy knew, the batman was the only close friend Uncle Walter ever talked about. Marie's intentions were good, but would Uncle Walter survive a few hours with Marie and a whisky bottle?

Amy hoped Henry went with her.

Amy mused that people criticised Marie all the time, but her heart was definitely in the right place.

Amy bit her lip. 'I'll phone him later. Try to reassure him. Uncle Walter was always very kind to me. He liked my dad a lot, and he kept in touch with me and my mother after Dad died, to make sure we were coping.'

Ben nodded. 'Marie said Uncle Walter is determined to visit you as soon as you can have visitors.' Ben kissed her forehead. 'I'm so glad that you're not seriously injured. That man could have killed you! We'll open a bottle of champagne and make plans. If the doctor gives the all clear, we could go out for a celebratory meal.'

'I'd rather spend a quiet night at the cottage with you, Ben!'

Ben said smoothly, 'That sounds fine to me. In fact it would be just about perfect.' He enjoyed the rush of colour to her cheeks.

The sister returned. 'The doctor is on his way, so it's time for you to wait

outside for a few minutes young man.'
Seeing Amy's flushed face and happy
expression, she continued. 'I can see
that you've done Amy a lot of good
already.'

Ben gave her a brilliant smile. 'I hope
so, she's my girl.'

The nurse studied them both, smiled
and nodded knowingly before she set
off down the ward.

He held Amy's hand. 'You are my
girl, Amy, aren't you? You will marry
me?'

She buried her lips against his hand
and looked up at him with an
expression that left him in no doubt.
'I'd love to, but perhaps you'll change
your mind when you know me better?'

Ben shook his head vigorously.
'Never!'

Eyes shining, Amy said, 'You've seen
me shrouded in dust, covered in paint,
and in shapeless working clothes. I do
look a lot better most of the time,
promise!'

He threw back his head and laughed.

'I know. You're a wonderful, determined, clever and beautiful woman. I can't believe my luck.' He ran his hand over his face. 'Mum has already decided you're perfect daughter-in-law material; she'll be absolutely delighted.'

'I hope so; I like your parents!'

'Good! I hope your mother will like me too. Oh . . . before I forget, there's one thing we should agree on now — dormer windows in the attic before the cottage is completely finished and before we have children.'

He managed to look sheepish before he added, 'It'll mean a bit more dust, I'm afraid!'

Her mouth dropped open, and he smiled wickedly before he added, 'But not too much, promise! And I'm a dab hand with the vacuum!' He got up when he noticed the doctor entering the ward. Placing a kiss on the palm of her hand that sent shivers down Amy's spine, he said, 'Back in a minute to take you home to your *Rose Cottage*.' He headed for the door and sent her another brilliant smile before he disappeared from view.

Looking back over the last couple of months, Amy decided Benjamin Tyler was decidedly a man who'd been worth a mountain of dust, muddled cables, confusing piping and a chequerboard of ditches. He definitely merited a couple of new dormer windows — dust or no dust!

THE END